GHOSTLY GRAPHIC ADVENTURES

DRAMA AT DUNGEON ROCK

Written by Baron Specter
Illustrated by Dustin Evans

visit us at www.abdopublishing.com

Published by Magic Wagon, a division of the ABDO Group, 8000 West 78th Street, Edina, Minnesota 55439. Copyright © 2011 by Abdo Consulting Group, Inc. International copyrights reserved in all countries. All rights reserved. No part of this book may be reproduced in any form without written permission from the publisher.

Graphic Planet™ is a trademark and logo of Magic Wagon.

Printed in the United States of America, North Mankato, Minnesota.
052010
092010
♻This book contains at least 10% recycled materials.

Written by Baron Specter
Illustrated by Dustin Evans
Lettered and designed by Ardden Entertainment LLC
Edited by Stephanie Hedlund and Rochelle Baltzer
Cover art by Dustin Evans
Cover design by Ardden Entertainment LLC

Library of Congress Cataloging-in-Publication Data

Specter, Baron, 1957-
   The sixth adventure : drama at Dungeon Rock / by Baron Specter ; illustrated by Dustin Evans.
       p. cm. -- (Ghostly graphic adventures)
   Summary: After spotting a mysterious ship while night fishing near Lynn, Massachusetts, Joey and Tank follow ghostly pirates into a cave that Joey's uncle tells them is rumored to hold a long-lost treasure.
   ISBN 978-1-60270-775-7
  1. Graphic novels. [1. Graphic novels. 2. Ghosts--Fiction. 3. Buried treasure--Fiction. 4. Pirates--Fiction. 5. Lynn (Mass.)--Fiction.] I. Evans, Dustin, 1982- ill. II. Title. III. Title: Drama at Dungeon Rock.
   PZ7.7.S648Six 2010
   741.5'973--dc22
                                   2009052895

TABLE OF CONTENTS

Our Heroes and Villains 4

Drama at Dungeon Rock 5

Dungeon Rock 31

Glossary 32

Web Sites 32

OUR HEROES AND VILLAINS

Joey DeAngelo
Hero

Uncle Mike
Hero

Tank
Hero

Thomas Veal
Villain

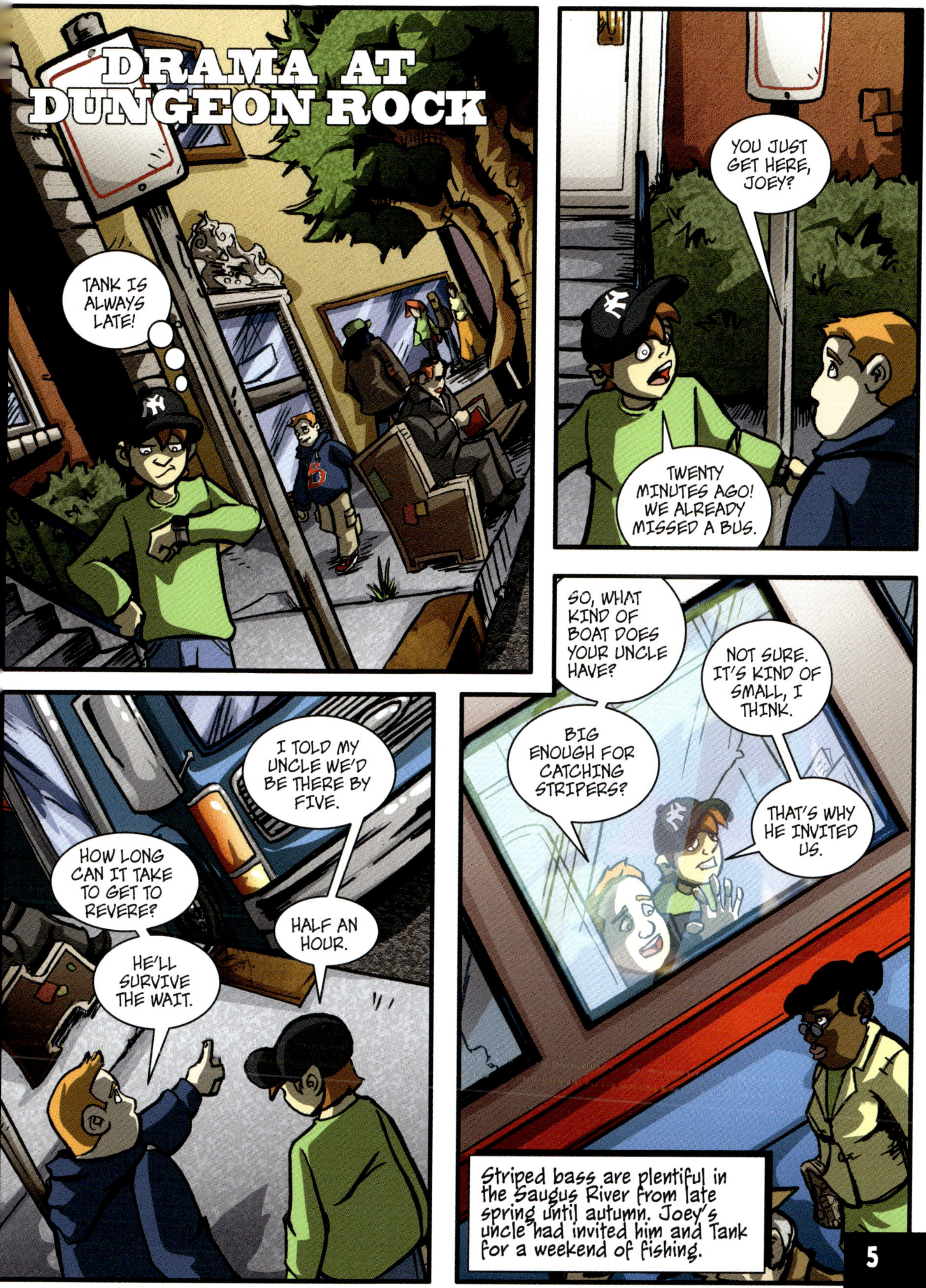

DRAMA AT DUNGEON ROCK
TANK IS ALWAYS LATE!
YOU JUST GET HERE, JOEY?
TWENTY MINUTES AGO! WE ALREADY MISSED A BUS.
I TOLD MY UNCLE WE'D BE THERE BY FIVE.
HOW LONG CAN IT TAKE TO GET TO REVERE?
HALF AN HOUR.
HE'LL SURVIVE THE WAIT.
SO, WHAT KIND OF BOAT DOES YOUR UNCLE HAVE?
NOT SURE. IT'S KIND OF SMALL, I THINK.
BIG ENOUGH FOR CATCHING STRIPERS?
THAT'S WHY HE INVITED US.
Striped bass are plentiful in the Saugus River from late spring until autumn. Joey's uncle had invited him and Tank for a weekend of fishing.

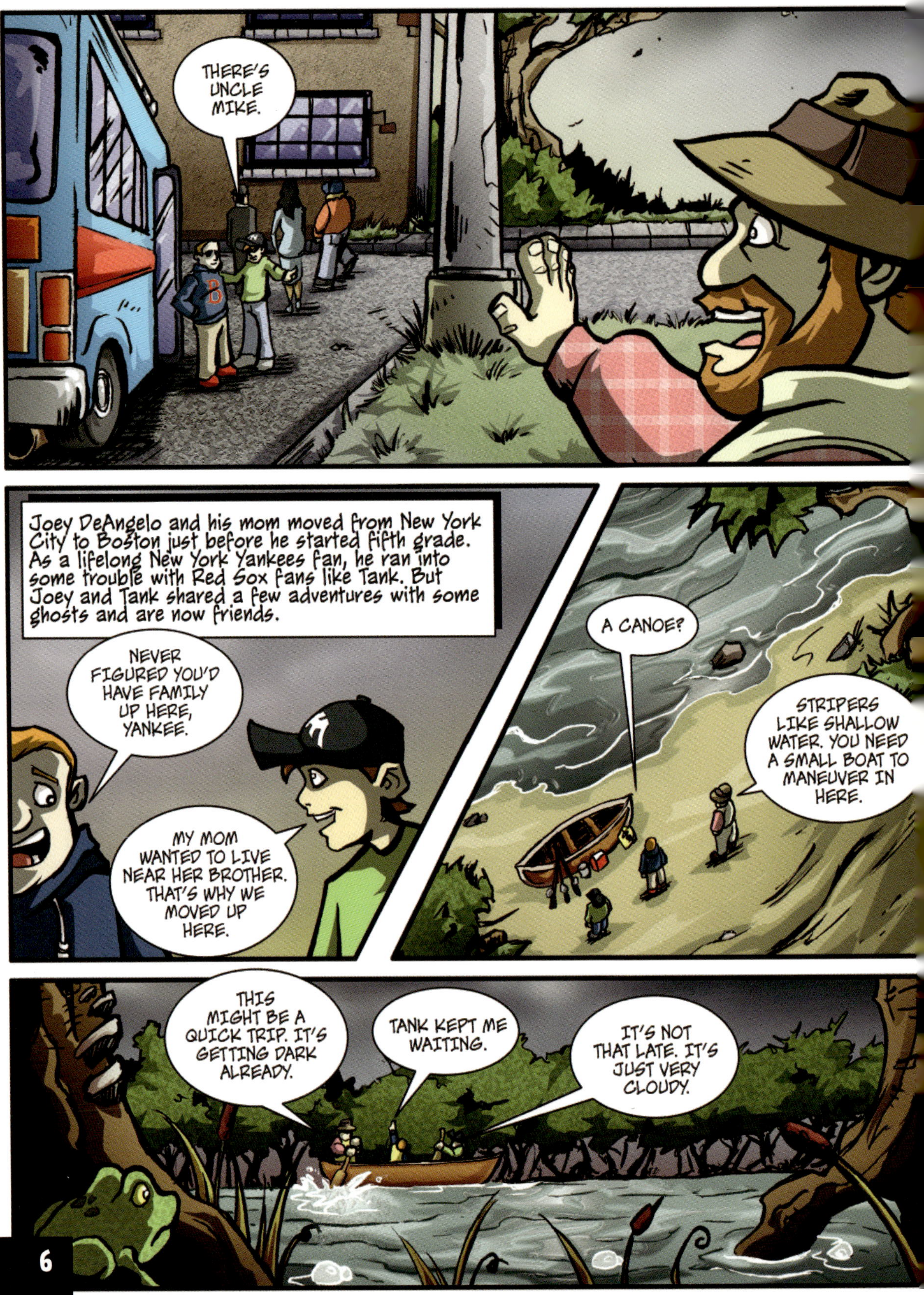
THERE'S UNCLE MIKE.
Joey DeAngelo and his mom moved from New York City to Boston just before he started fifth grade. As a lifelong New York Yankees fan, he ran into some trouble with Red Sox fans like Tank. But Joey and Tank shared a few adventures with some ghosts and are now friends.
NEVER FIGURED YOU'D HAVE FAMILY UP HERE, YANKEE.
MY MOM WANTED TO LIVE NEAR HER BROTHER. THAT'S WHY WE MOVED UP HERE.
A CANOE?
STRIPERS LIKE SHALLOW WATER. YOU NEED A SMALL BOAT TO MANEUVER IN HERE.
THIS MIGHT BE A QUICK TRIP. IT'S GETTING DARK ALREADY.
TANK KEPT ME WAITING.
IT'S NOT THAT LATE. IT'S JUST VERY CLOUDY.

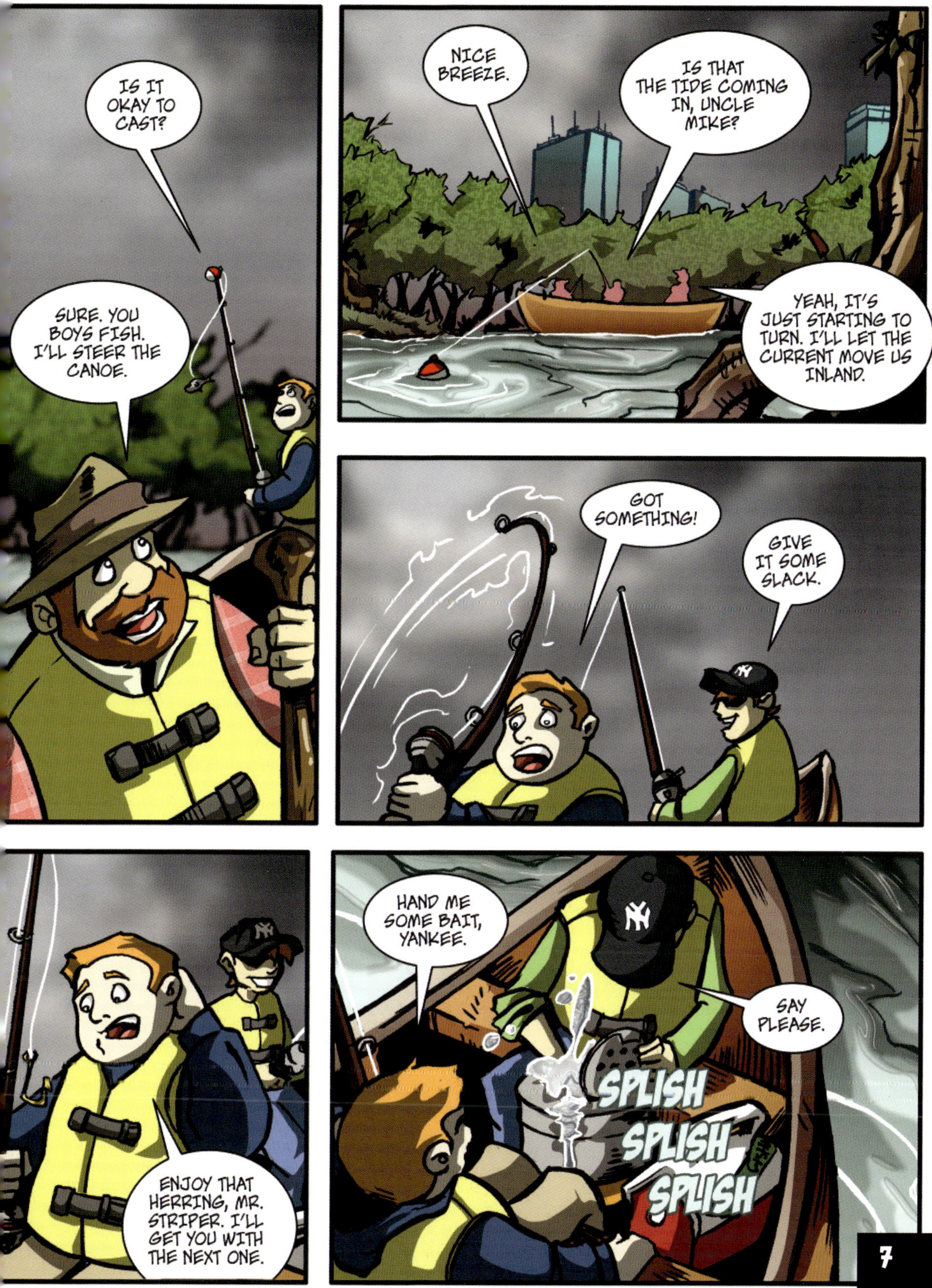
IS IT OKAY TO CAST?
SURE. YOU BOYS FISH. I'LL STEER THE CANOE.
NICE BREEZE.
IS THAT THE TIDE COMING IN, UNCLE MIKE?
YEAH, IT'S JUST STARTING TO TURN. I'LL LET THE CURRENT MOVE US INLAND.
GOT SOMETHING!
GIVE IT SOME SLACK.
ENJOY THAT HERRING, MR. STRIPER. I'LL GET YOU WITH THE NEXT ONE.
HAND ME SOME BAIT, YANKEE.
SAY PLEASE.
SPLISH
SPLISH
SPLISH

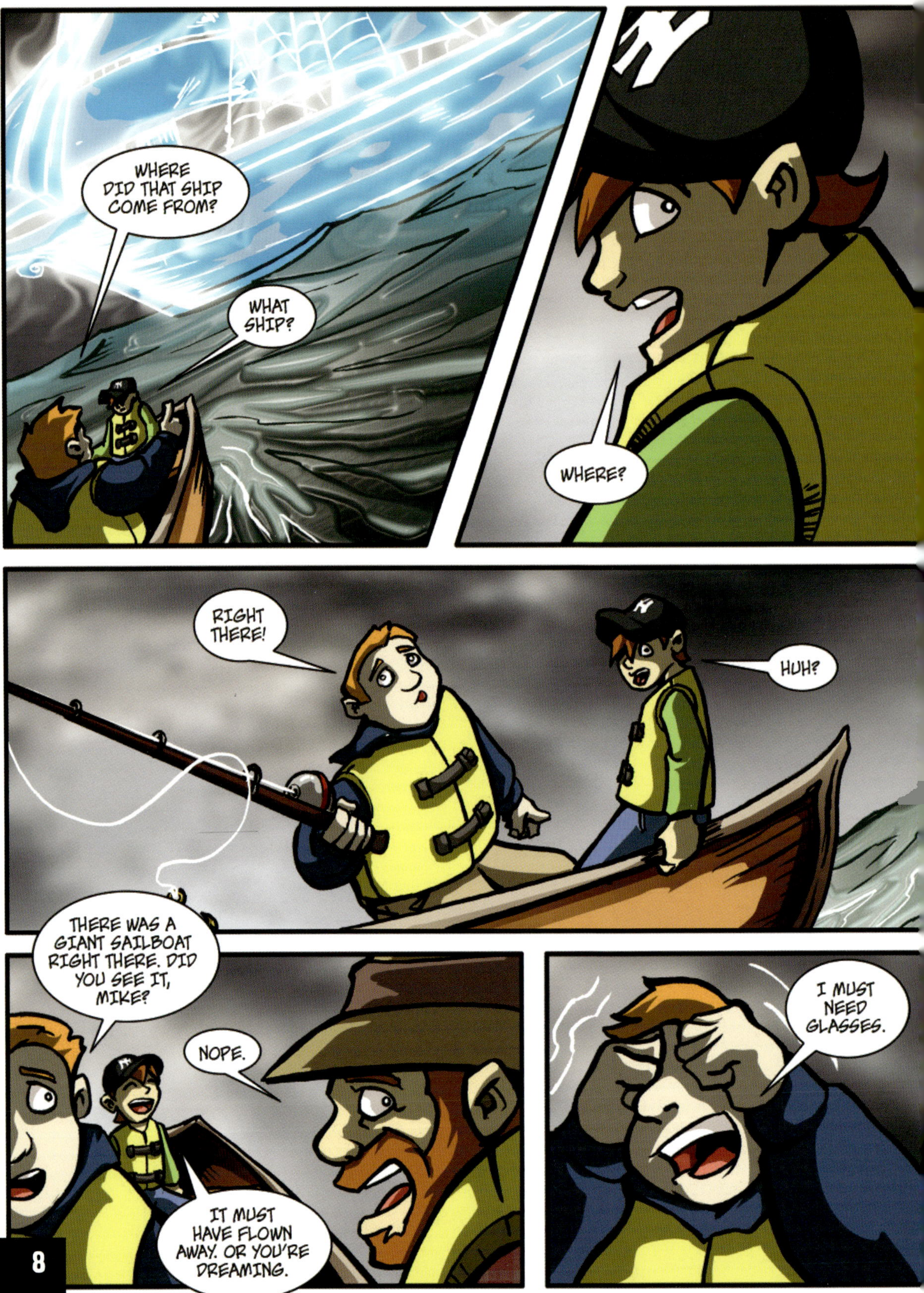
WHERE DID THAT SHIP COME FROM?
WHAT SHIP?
WHERE?
RIGHT THERE!
HUH?
THERE WAS A GIANT SAILBOAT RIGHT THERE. DID YOU SEE IT, MIKE?
NOPE.
IT MUST HAVE FLOWN AWAY. OR YOU'RE DREAMING.
I MUST NEED GLASSES.

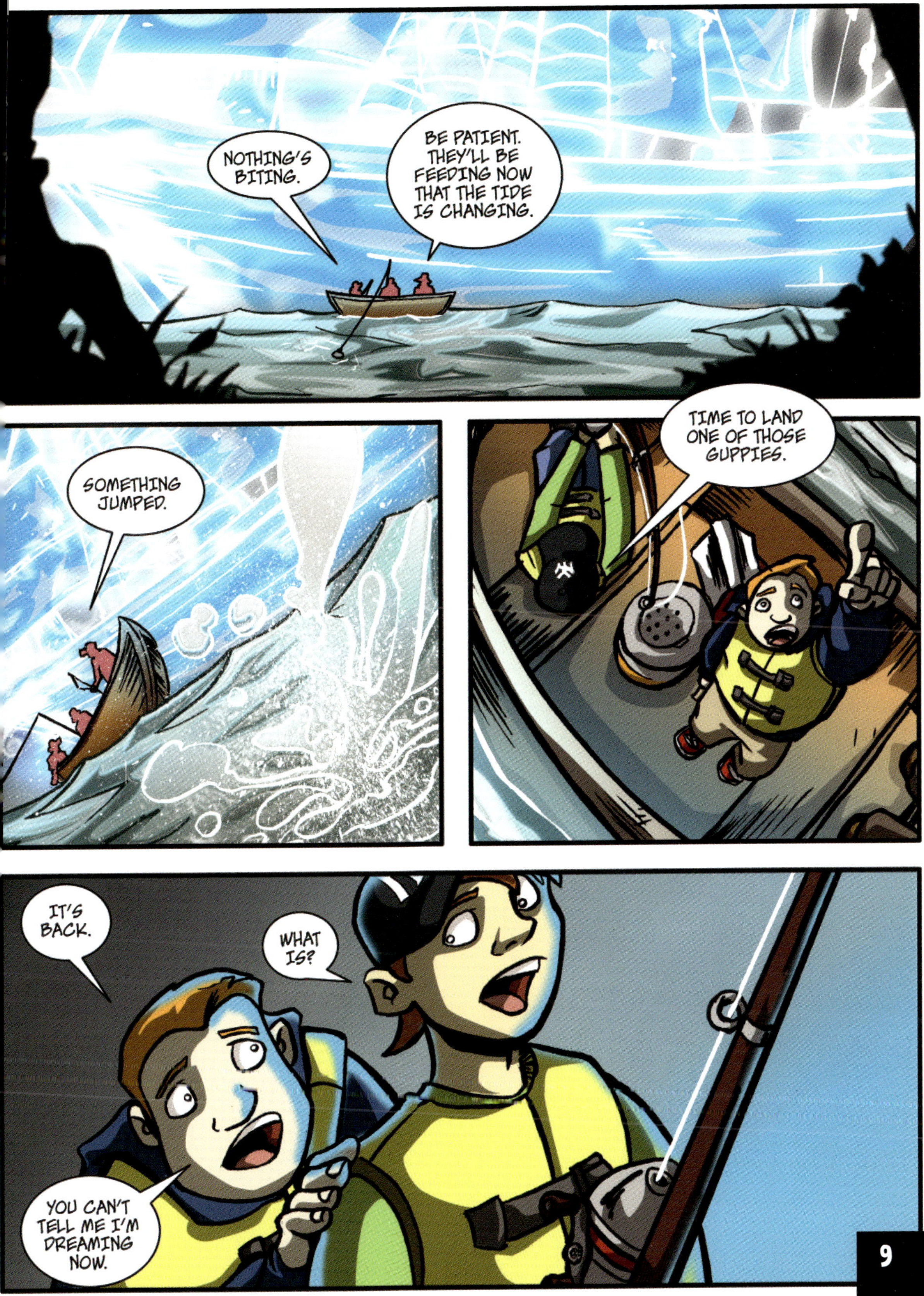
NOTHING'S BITING.
BE PATIENT. THEY'LL BE FEEDING NOW THAT THE TIDE IS CHANGING.
SOMETHING JUMPED.
TIME TO LAND ONE OF THOSE GUPPIES.
IT'S BACK.
WHAT IS?
YOU CAN'T TELL ME I'M DREAMING NOW.

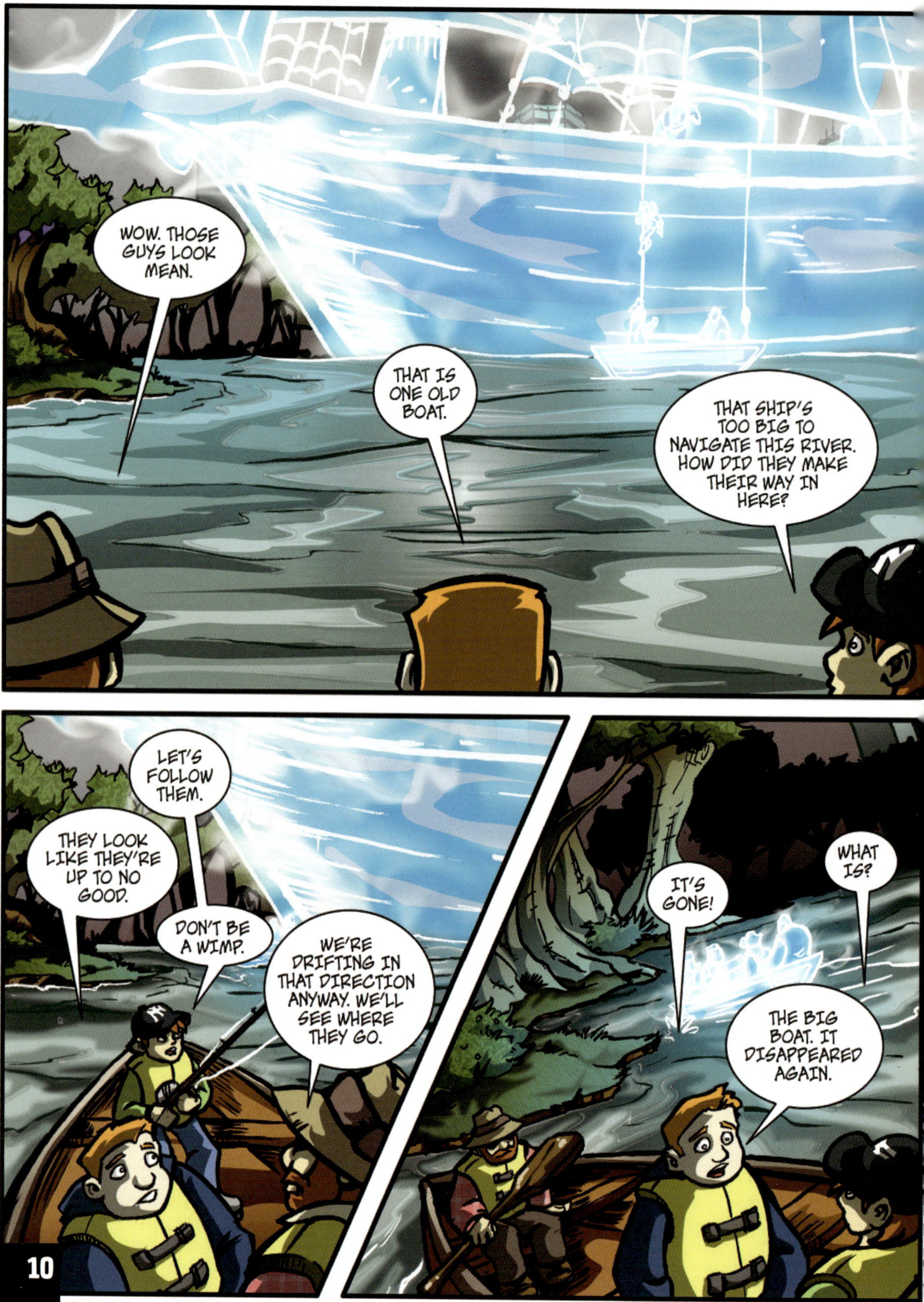
WOW. THOSE GUYS LOOK MEAN.
THAT IS ONE OLD BOAT.
THAT SHIP'S TOO BIG TO NAVIGATE THIS RIVER. HOW DID THEY MAKE THEIR WAY IN HERE?
LET'S FOLLOW THEM.
THEY LOOK LIKE THEY'RE UP TO NO GOOD.
DON'T BE A WIMP.
WE'RE DRIFTING IN THAT DIRECTION ANYWAY. WE'LL SEE WHERE THEY GO.
IT'S GONE!
WHAT IS?
THE BIG BOAT. IT DISAPPEARED AGAIN.

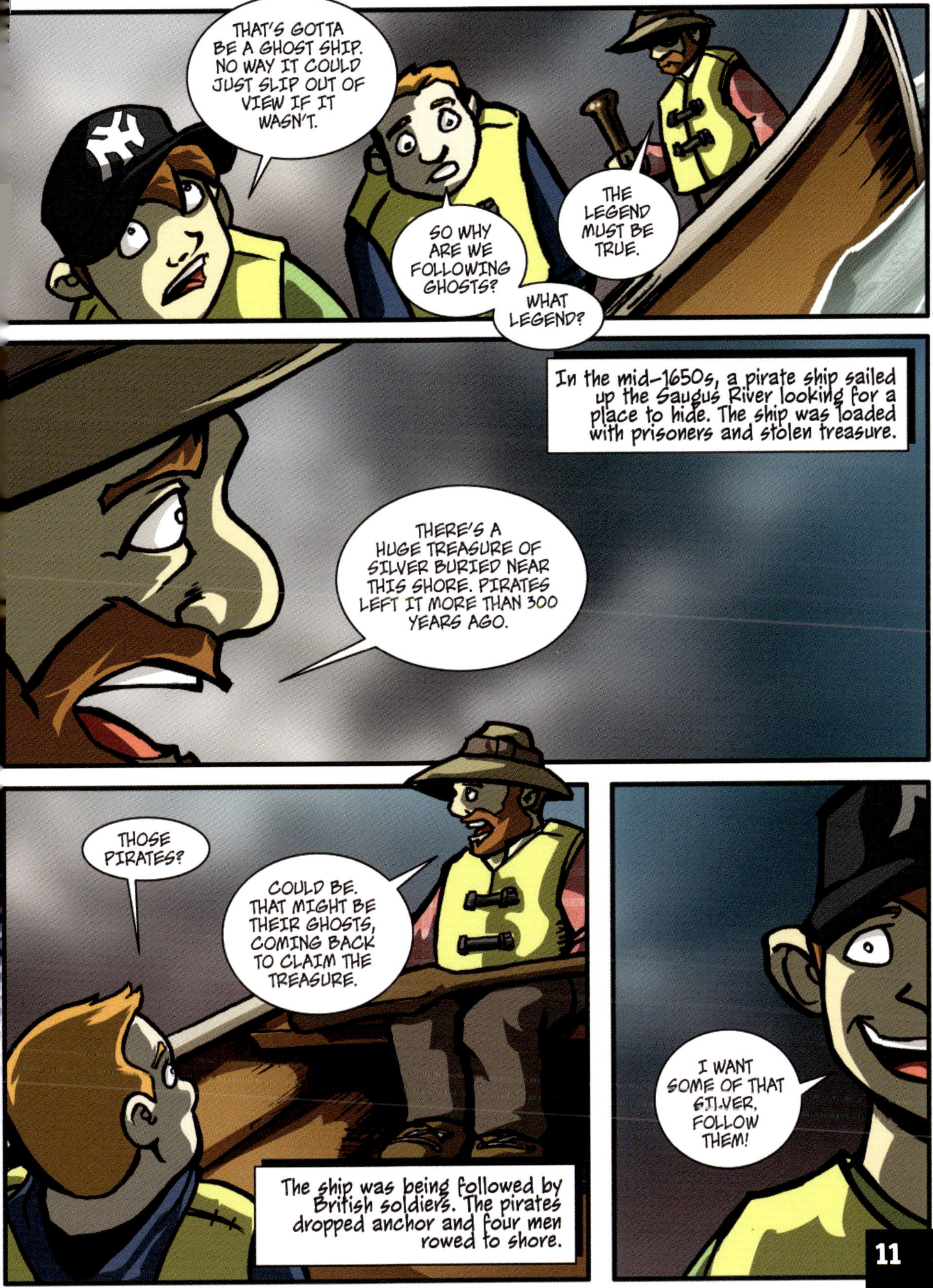
THAT'S GOTTA BE A GHOST SHIP. NO WAY IT COULD JUST SLIP OUT OF VIEW IF IT WASN'T.
SO WHY ARE WE FOLLOWING GHOSTS?
THE LEGEND MUST BE TRUE.
WHAT LEGEND?
In the mid-1650s, a pirate ship sailed up the Saugus River looking for a place to hide. The ship was loaded with prisoners and stolen treasure.
THERE'S A HUGE TREASURE OF SILVER BURIED NEAR THIS SHORE. PIRATES LEFT IT MORE THAN 300 YEARS AGO.
THOSE PIRATES?
COULD BE. THAT MIGHT BE THEIR GHOSTS, COMING BACK TO CLAIM THE TREASURE.
The ship was being followed by British soldiers. The pirates dropped anchor and four men rowed to shore.
I WANT SOME OF THAT SILVER. FOLLOW THEM!

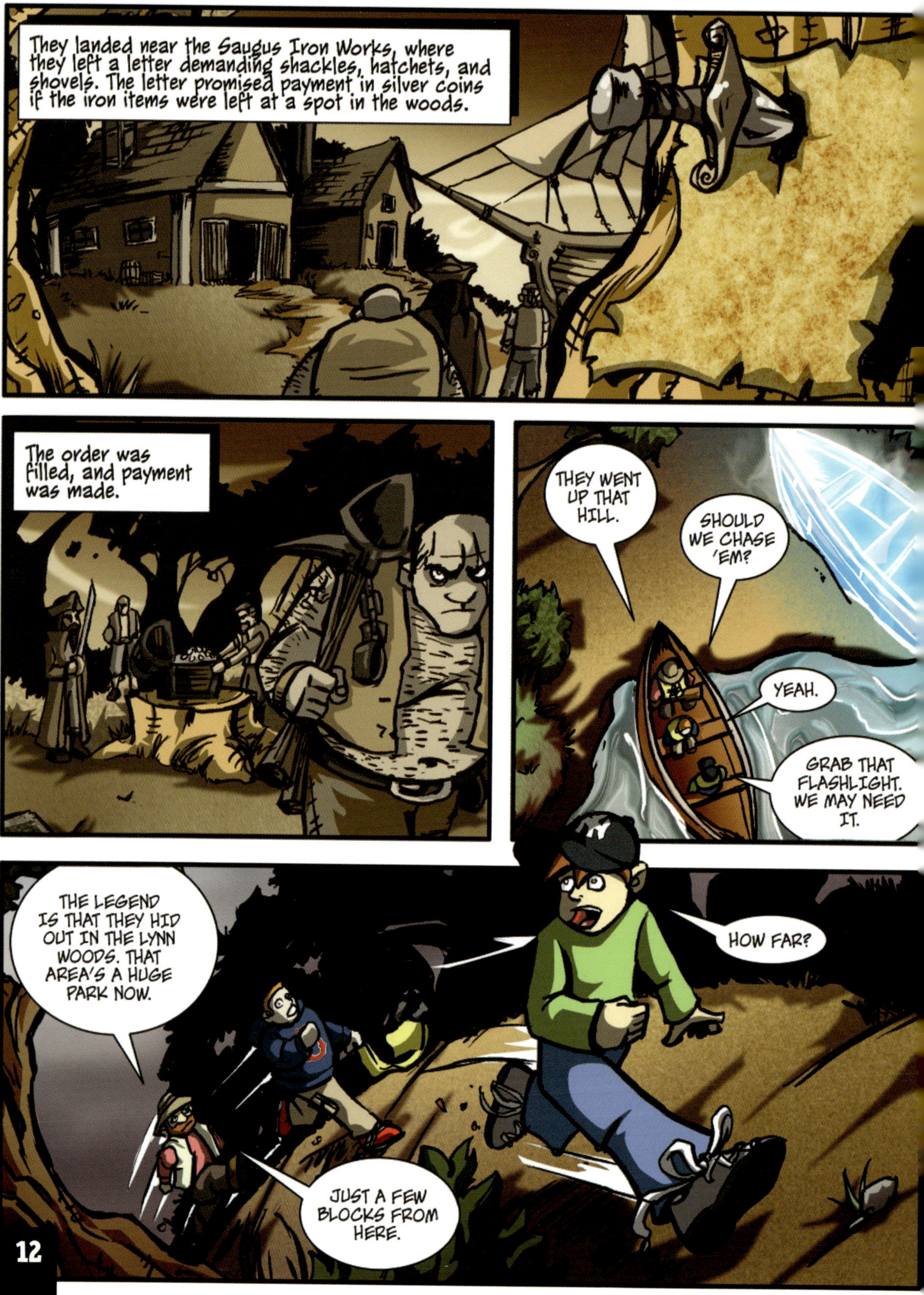
They landed near the Saugus Iron Works, where they left a letter demanding shackles, hatchets, and shovels. The letter promised payment in silver coins if the iron items were left at a spot in the woods.
The order was filled, and payment was made.
THEY WENT UP THAT HILL.
SHOULD WE CHASE 'EM?
YEAH.
GRAB THAT FLASHLIGHT. WE MAY NEED IT.
THE LEGEND IS THAT THEY HID OUT IN THE LYNN WOODS. THAT AREA'S A HUGE PARK NOW.
HOW FAR?
JUST A FEW BLOCKS FROM HERE.

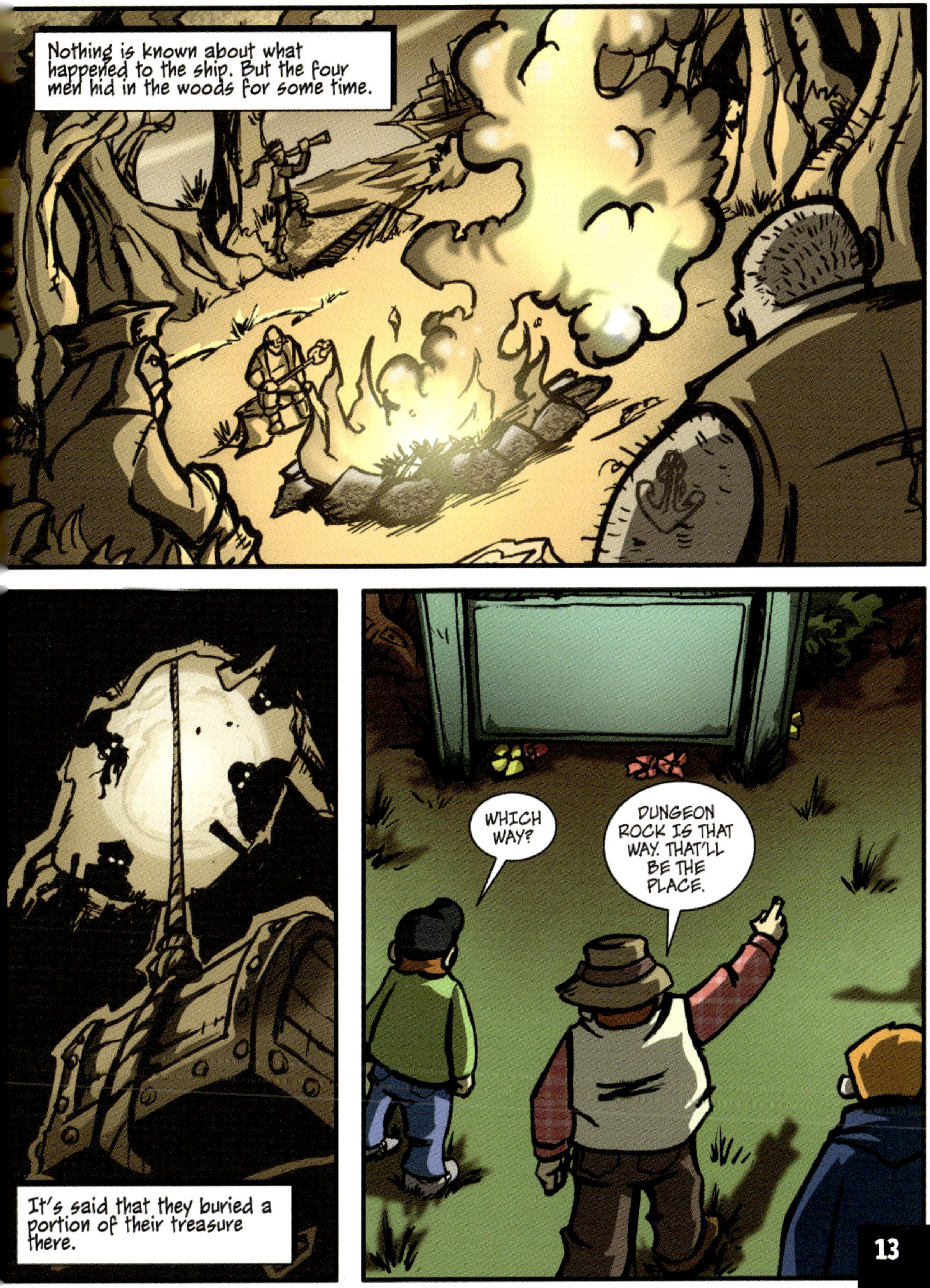
Nothing is known about what happened to the ship. But the four men hid in the woods for some time.
It's said that they buried a portion of their treasure there.
WHICH WAY?
DUNGEON ROCK IS THAT WAY. THAT'LL BE THE PLACE.

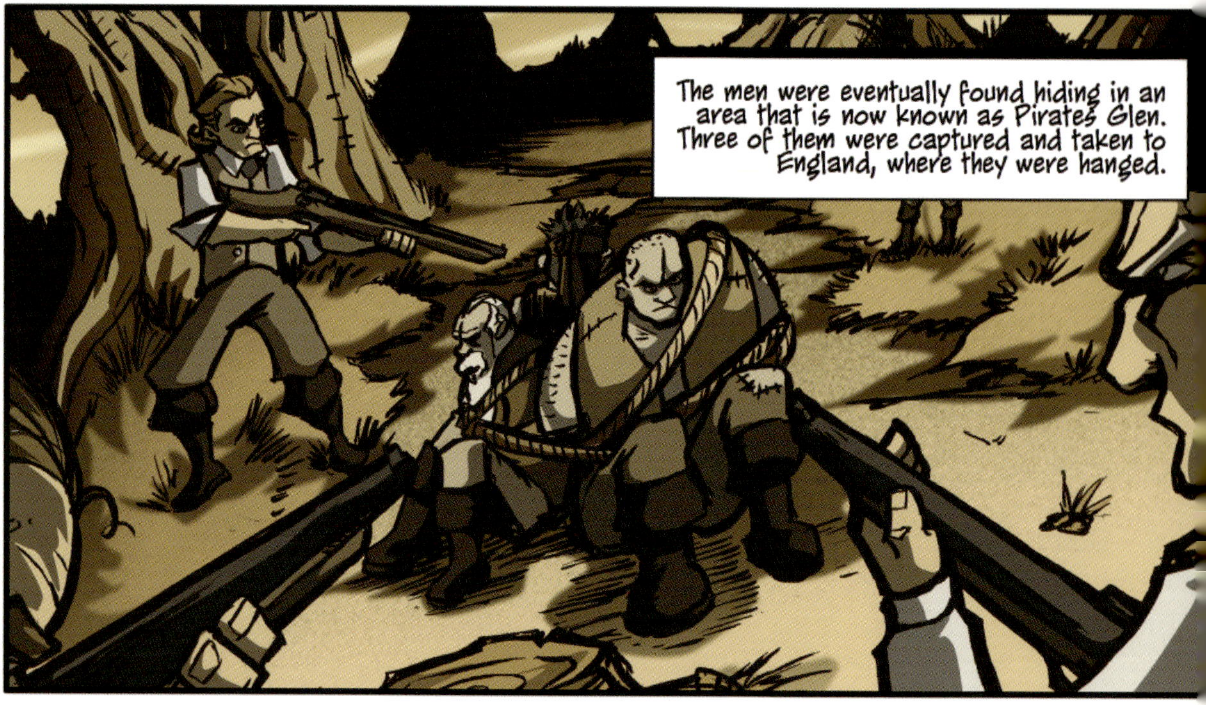
The men were eventually found hiding in an area that is now known as Pirates Glen. Three of them were captured and taken to England, where they were hanged.

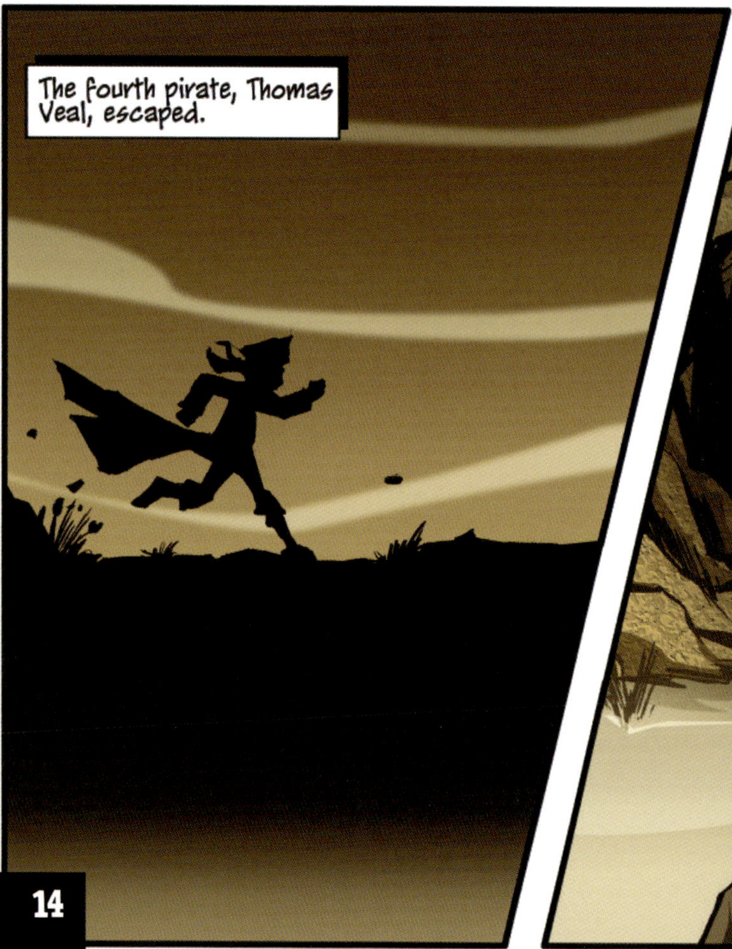
The fourth pirate, Thomas Veal, escaped.

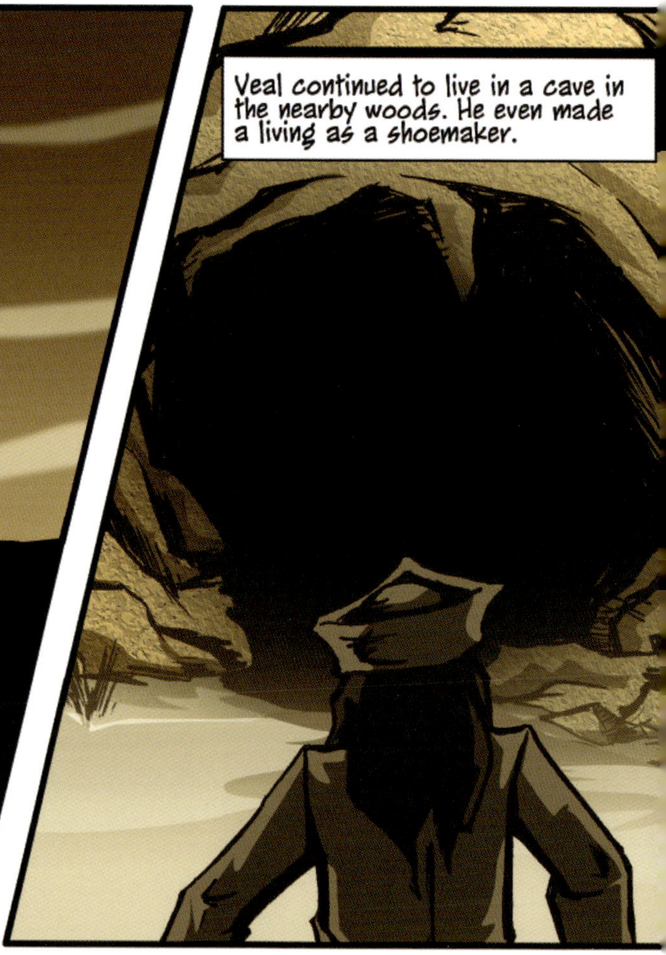
Veal continued to live in a cave in the nearby woods. He even made a living as a shoemaker.

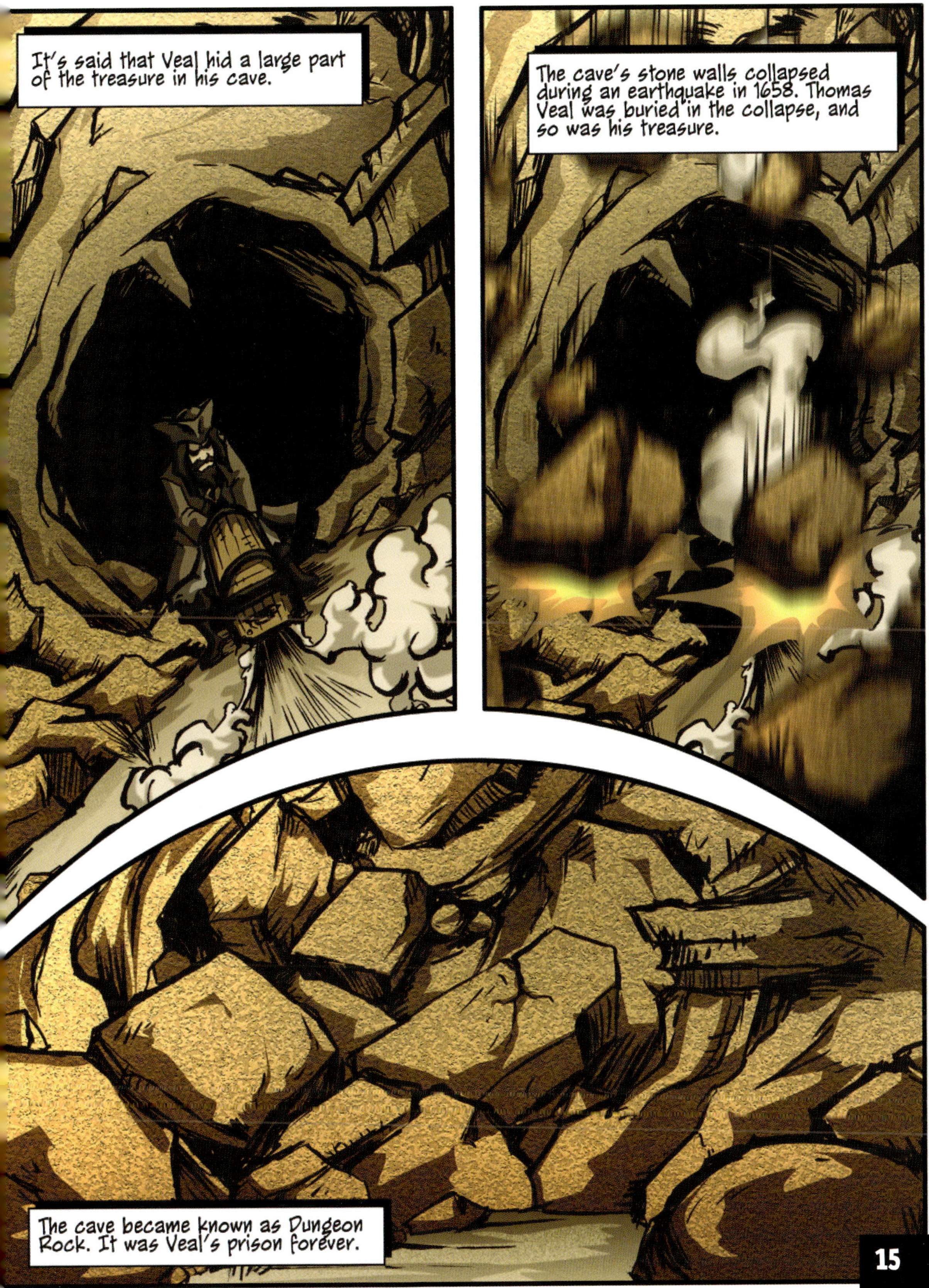
It's said that Veal hid a large part of the treasure in his cave.
The cave's stone walls collapsed during an earthquake in 1658. Thomas Veal was buried in the collapse, and so was his treasure.
The cave became known as Dungeon Rock. It was Veal's prison forever.

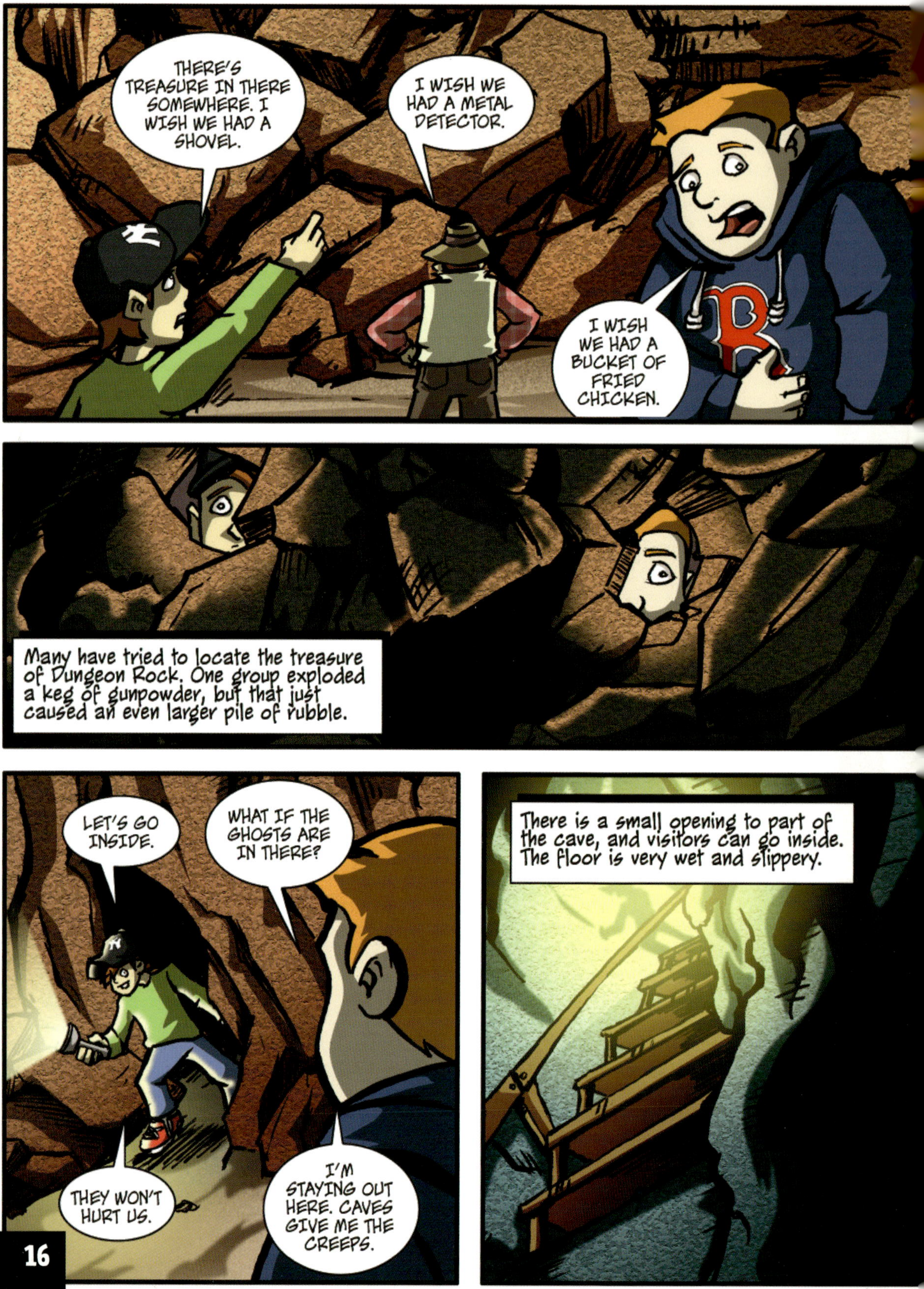
THERE'S TREASURE IN THERE SOMEWHERE. I WISH WE HAD A SHOVEL.
I WISH WE HAD A METAL DETECTOR.
I WISH WE HAD A BUCKET OF FRIED CHICKEN.
Many have tried to locate the treasure of Dungeon Rock. One group exploded a keg of gunpowder, but that just caused an even larger pile of rubble.
LET'S GO INSIDE.
WHAT IF THE GHOSTS ARE IN THERE?
THEY WON'T HURT US.
I'M STAYING OUT HERE. CAVES GIVE ME THE CREEPS.
There is a small opening to part of the cave, and visitors can go inside. The floor is very wet and slippery.

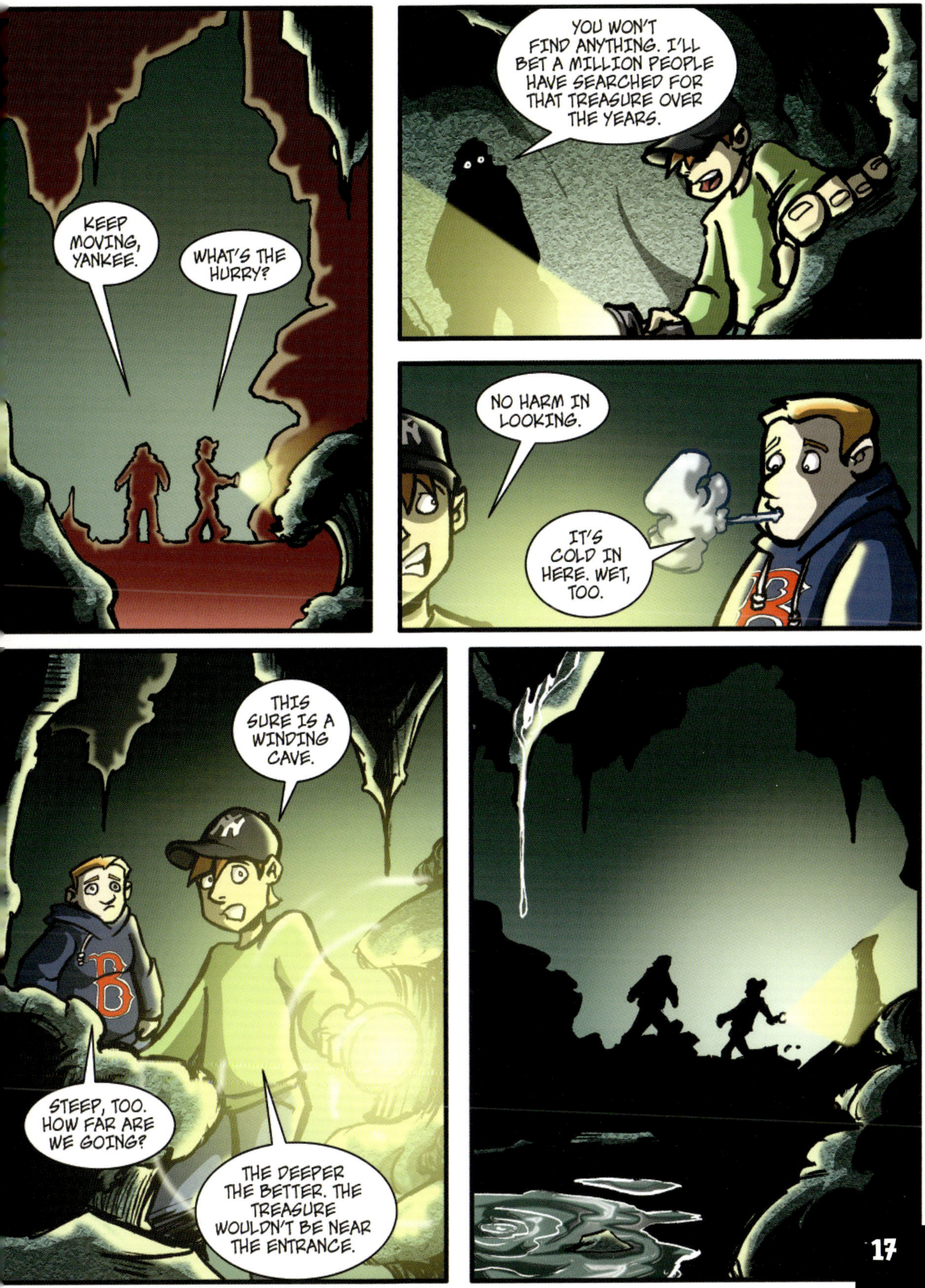
KEEP MOVING, YANKEE.
WHAT'S THE HURRY?
YOU WON'T FIND ANYTHING. I'LL BET A MILLION PEOPLE HAVE SEARCHED FOR THAT TREASURE OVER THE YEARS.
NO HARM IN LOOKING.
IT'S COLD IN HERE. WET, TOO.
THIS SURE IS A WINDING CAVE.
STEEP, TOO. HOW FAR ARE WE GOING?
THE DEEPER THE BETTER. THE TREASURE WOULDN'T BE NEAR THE ENTRANCE.

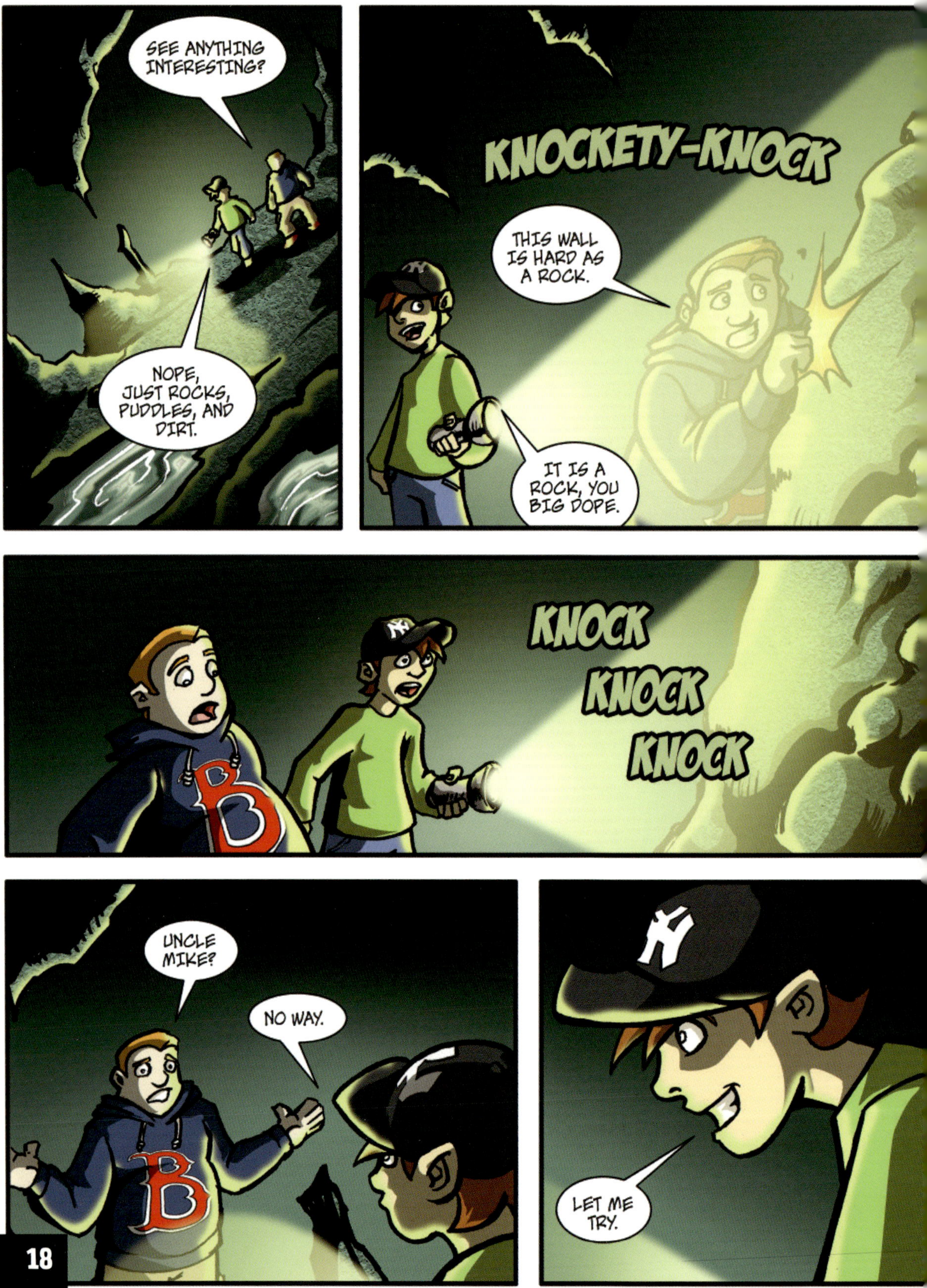
SEE ANYTHING INTERESTING?
NOPE, JUST ROCKS, PUDDLES, AND DIRT.
KNOCKETY-KNOCK
THIS WALL IS HARD AS A ROCK.
IT IS A ROCK, YOU BIG DOPE.
KNOCK
KNOCK
KNOCK
UNCLE MIKE?
NO WAY.
LET ME TRY.

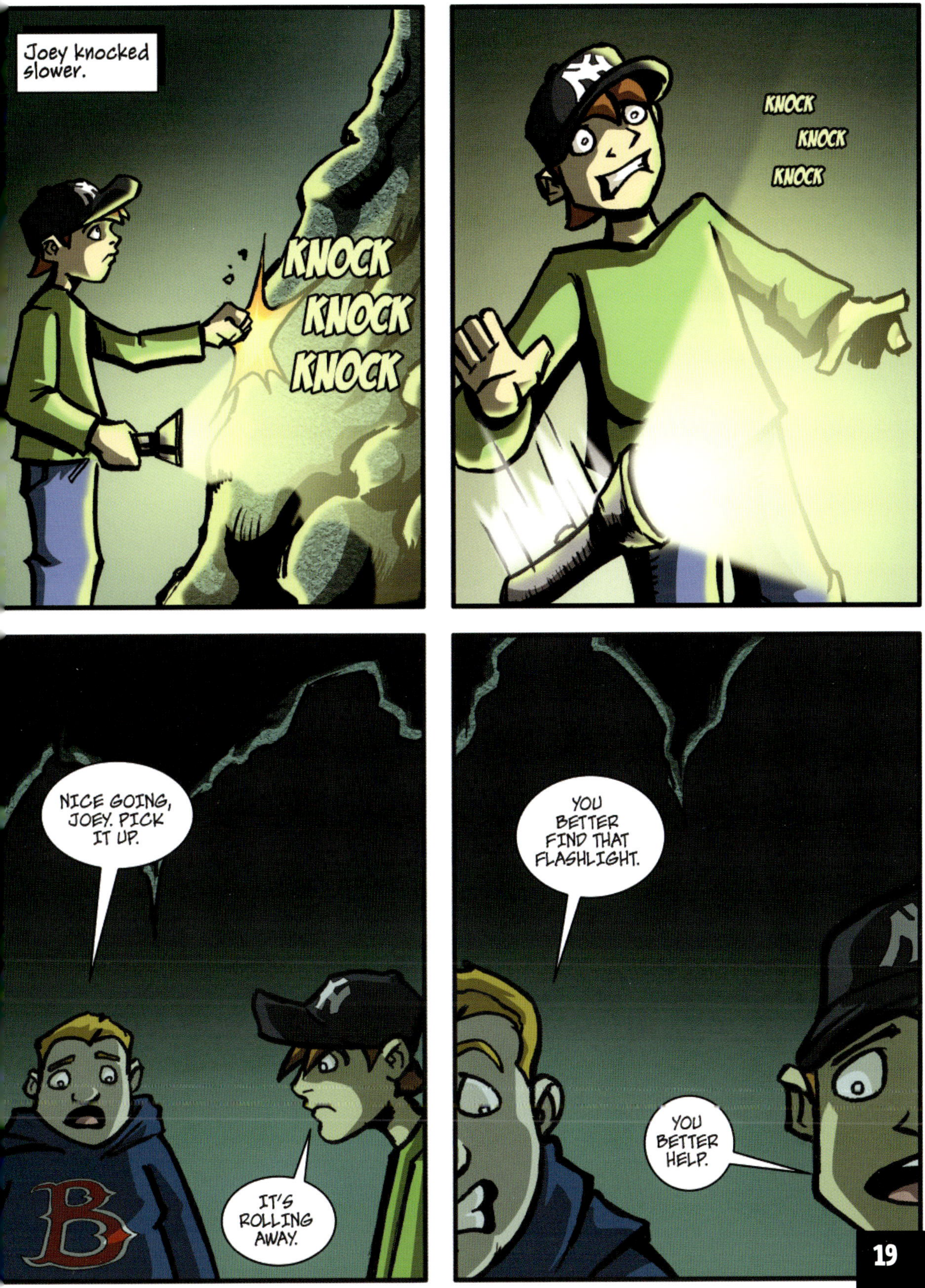
Joey knocked slower.
KNOCK KNOCK KNOCK
KNOCK KNOCK KNOCK
NICE GOING, JOEY. PICK IT UP.
IT'S ROLLING AWAY.
YOU BETTER FIND THAT FLASHLIGHT.
YOU BETTER HELP.

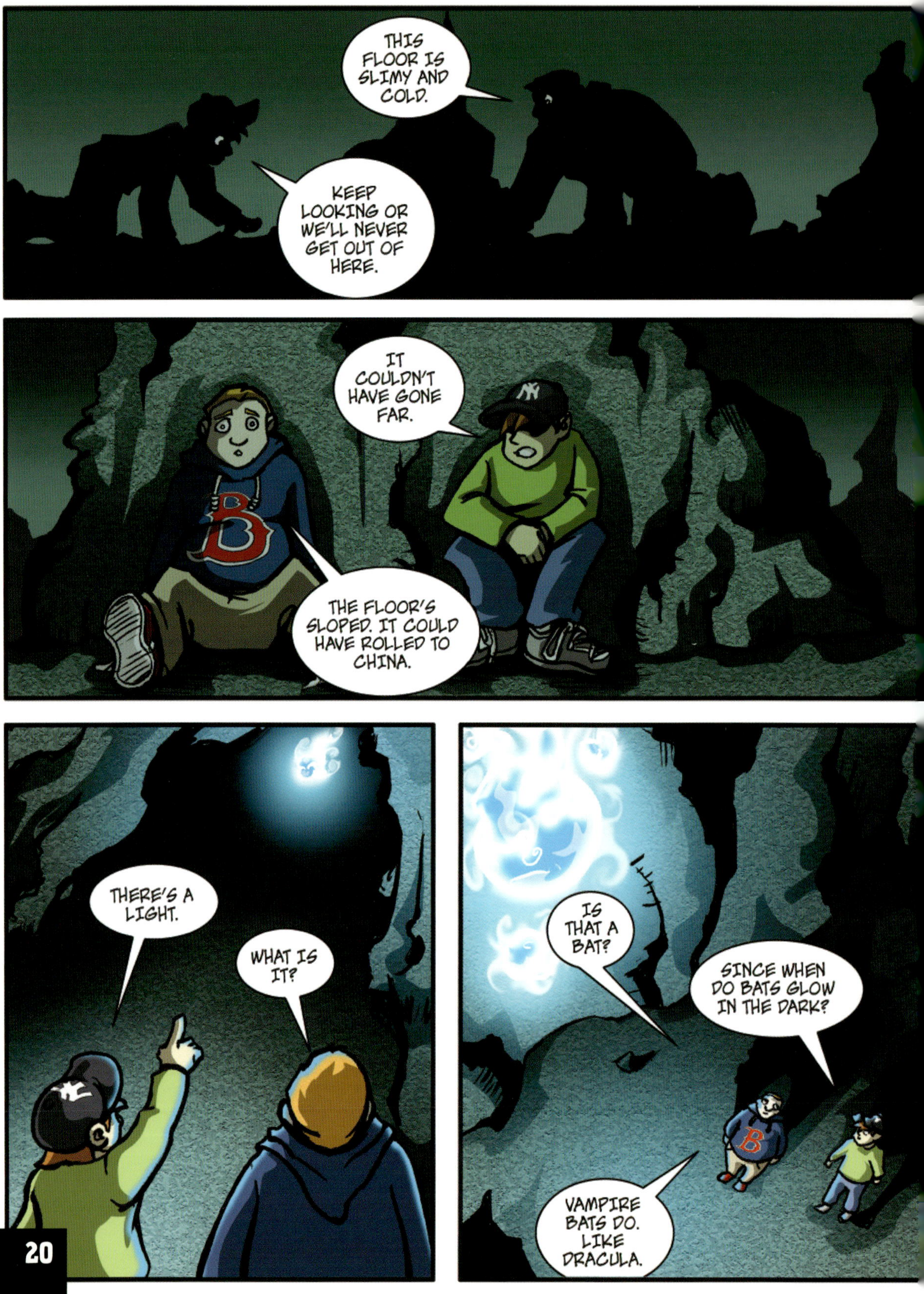

THIS FLOOR IS SLIMY AND COLD.
KEEP LOOKING OR WE'LL NEVER GET OUT OF HERE.
IT COULDN'T HAVE GONE FAR.
THE FLOOR'S SLOPED. IT COULD HAVE ROLLED TO CHINA.
THERE'S A LIGHT.
WHAT IS IT?
IS THAT A BAT?
SINCE WHEN DO BATS GLOW IN THE DARK?
VAMPIRE BATS DO. LIKE DRACULA.

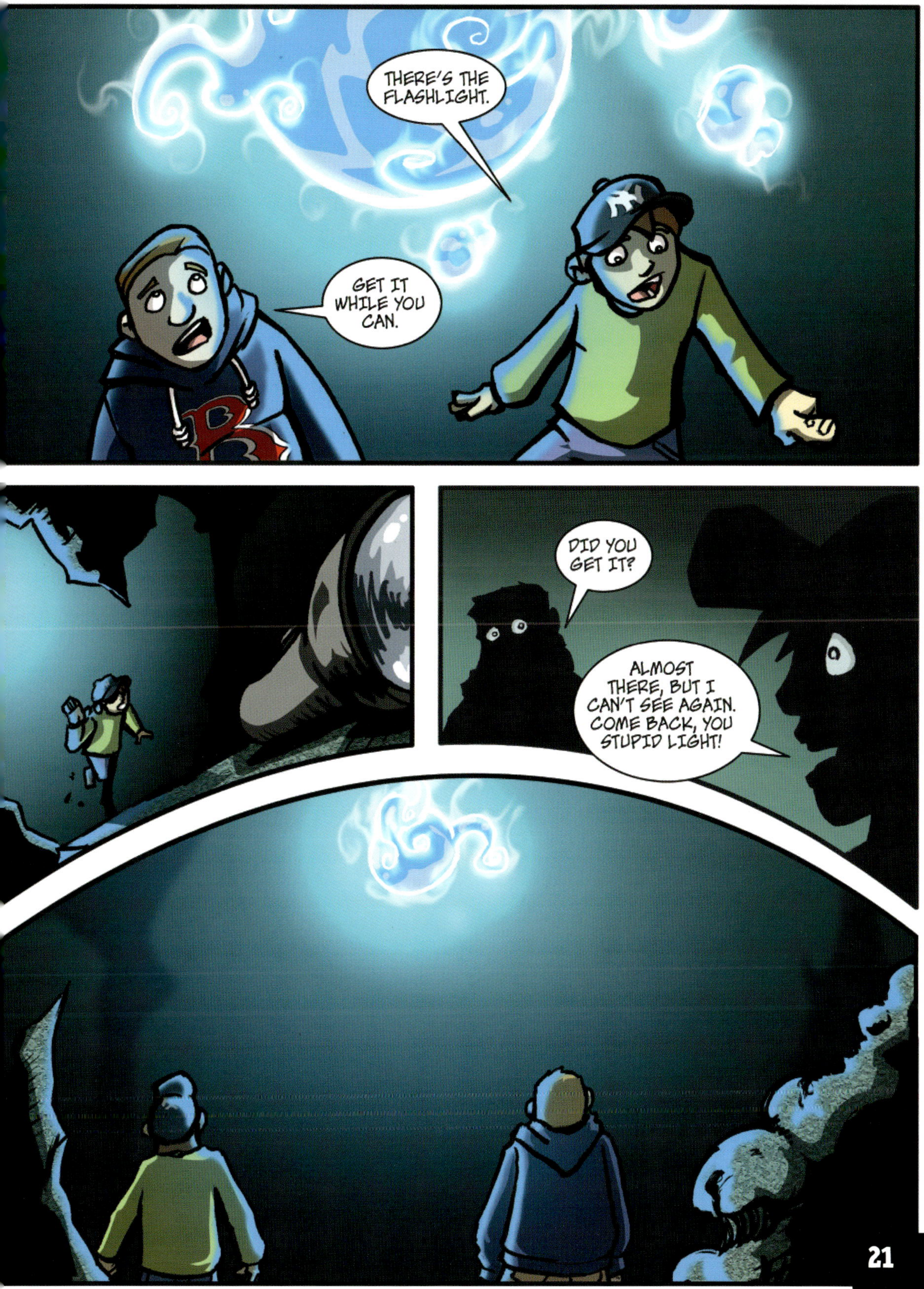
THERE'S THE FLASHLIGHT.
GET IT WHILE YOU CAN.
DID YOU GET IT?
ALMOST THERE, BUT I CAN'T SEE AGAIN. COME BACK, YOU STUPID LIGHT!

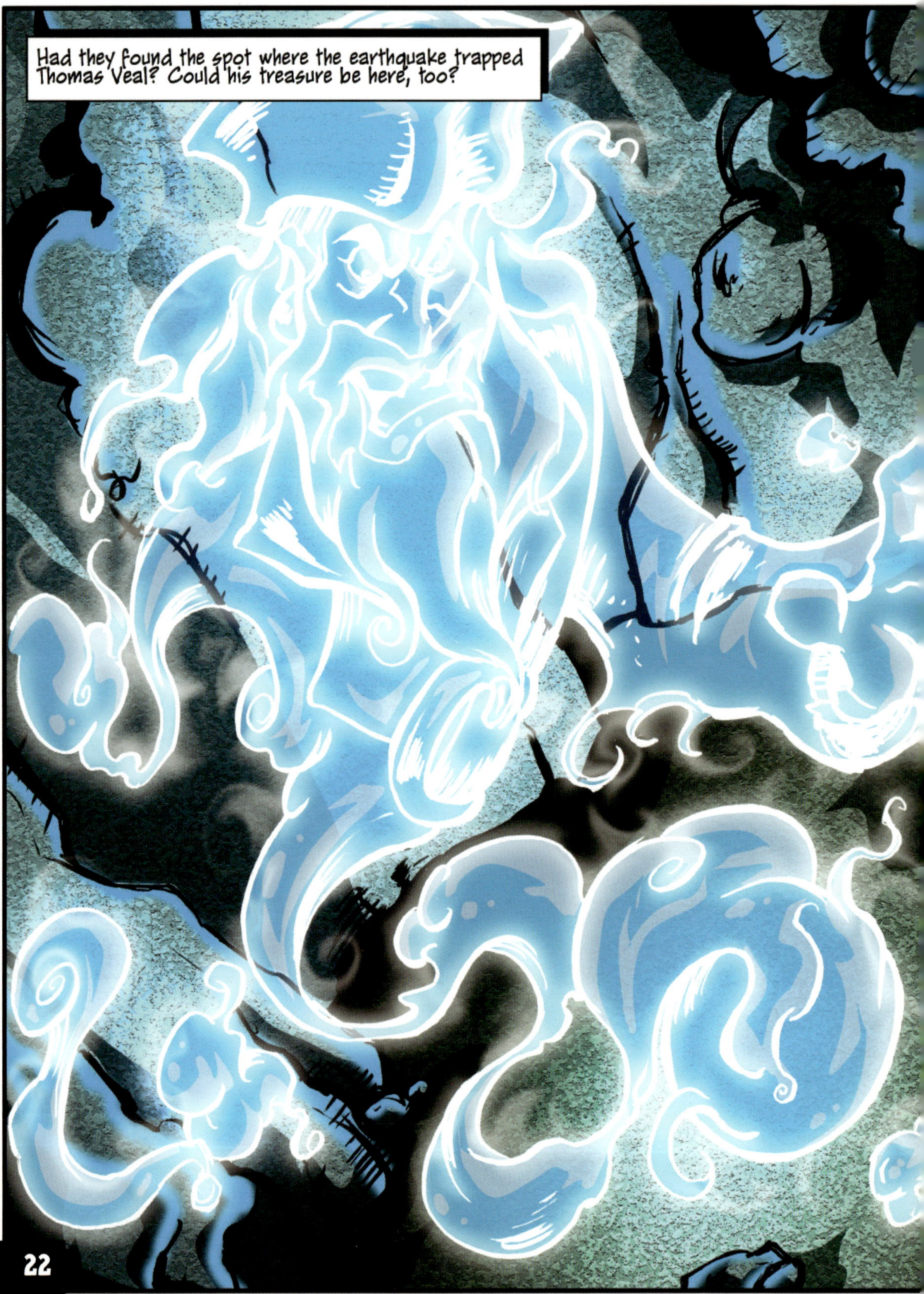
Had they found the spot where the earthquake trapped Thomas Veal? Could his treasure be here, too?

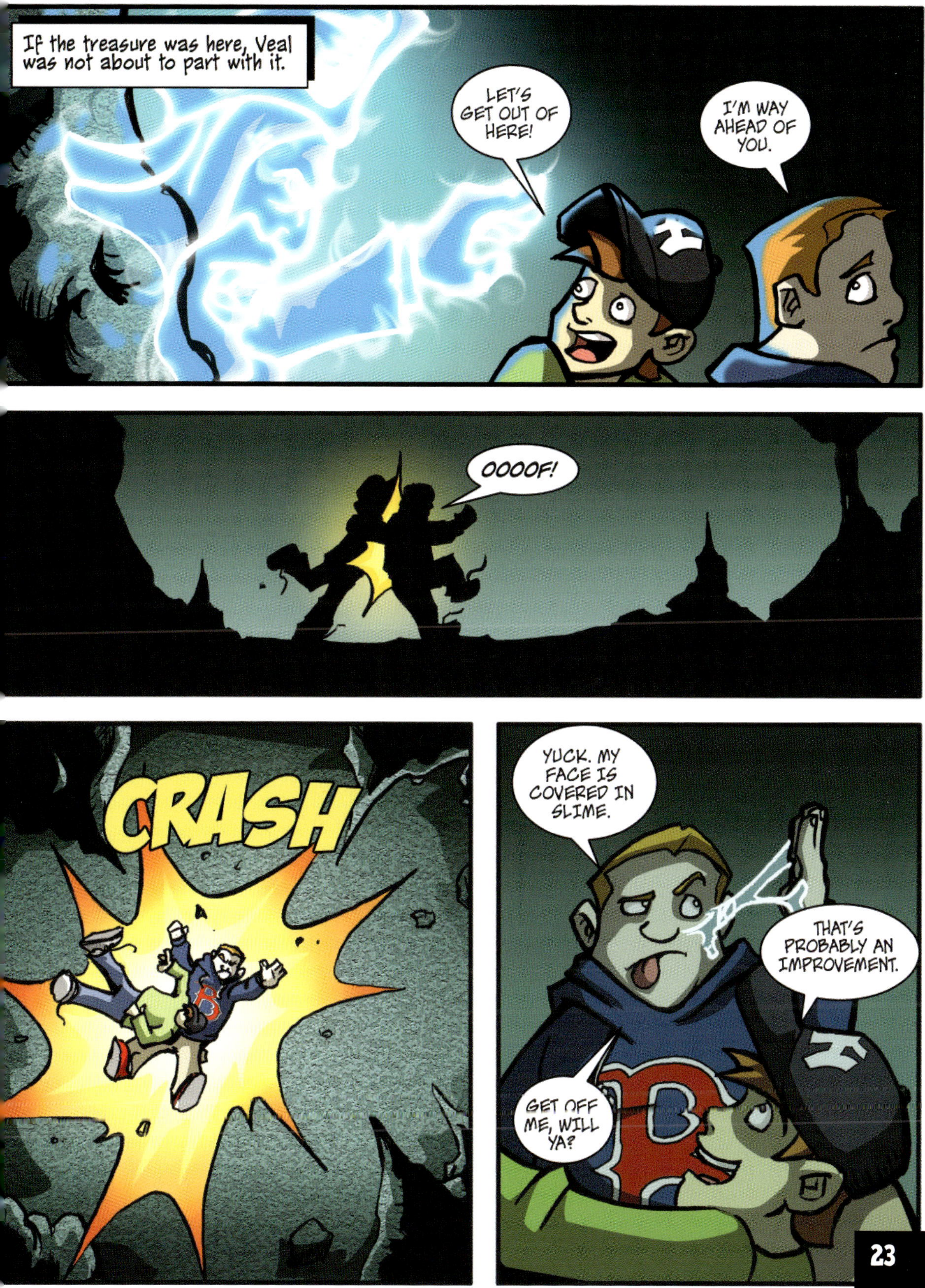
If the treasure was here, Veal was not about to part with it.
LET'S GET OUT OF HERE!
I'M WAY AHEAD OF YOU.
OOOOF!
CRASH
YUCK. MY FACE IS COVERED IN SLIME.
THAT'S PROBABLY AN IMPROVEMENT.
GET OFF ME, WILL YA?

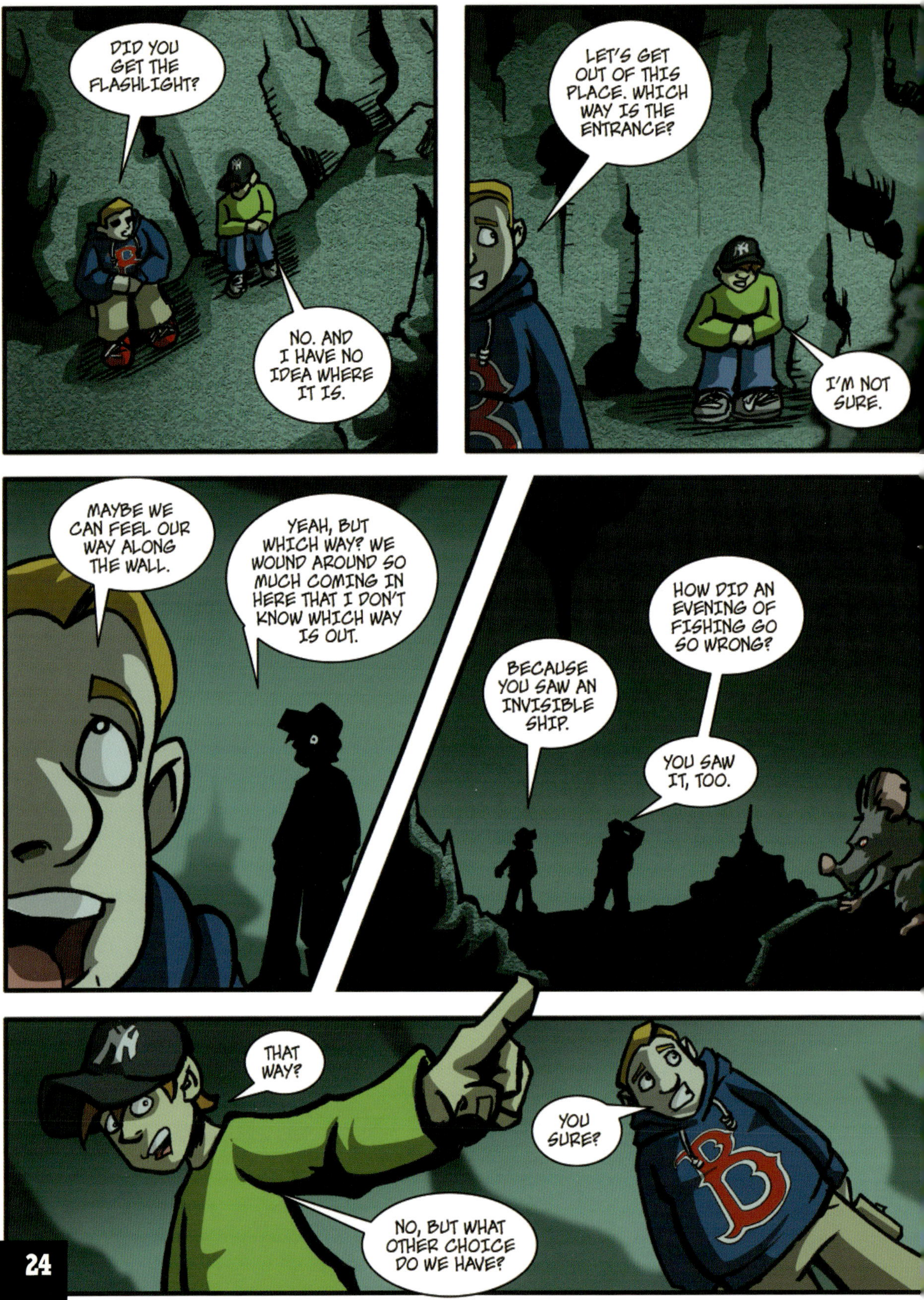
DID YOU GET THE FLASHLIGHT?
NO. AND I HAVE NO IDEA WHERE IT IS.
LET'S GET OUT OF THIS PLACE. WHICH WAY IS THE ENTRANCE?
I'M NOT SURE.
MAYBE WE CAN FEEL OUR WAY ALONG THE WALL.
YEAH, BUT WHICH WAY? WE WOUND AROUND SO MUCH COMING IN HERE THAT I DON'T KNOW WHICH WAY IS OUT.
HOW DID AN EVENING OF FISHING GO SO WRONG?
BECAUSE YOU SAW AN INVISIBLE SHIP.
YOU SAW IT, TOO.
THAT WAY?
YOU SURE?
NO, BUT WHAT OTHER CHOICE DO WE HAVE?

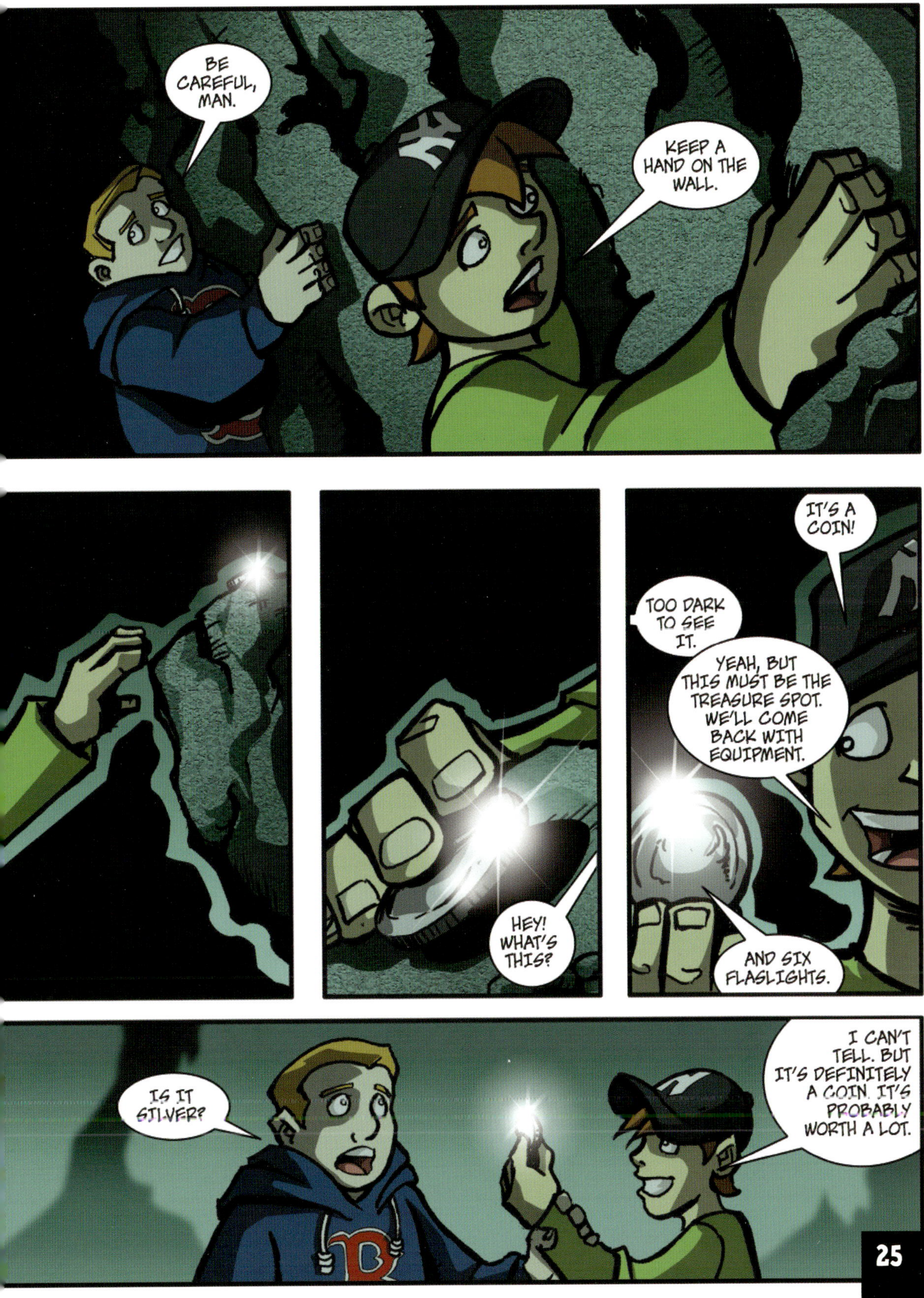
BE CAREFUL, MAN.
KEEP A HAND ON THE WALL.
HEY! WHAT'S THIS?
IT'S A COIN!
TOO DARK TO SEE IT.
YEAH, BUT THIS MUST BE THE TREASURE SPOT. WE'LL COME BACK WITH EQUIPMENT.
AND SIX FLASLIGHTS.
IS IT SILVER?
I CAN'T TELL. BUT IT'S DEFINITELY A COIN. IT'S PROBABLY WORTH A LOT.

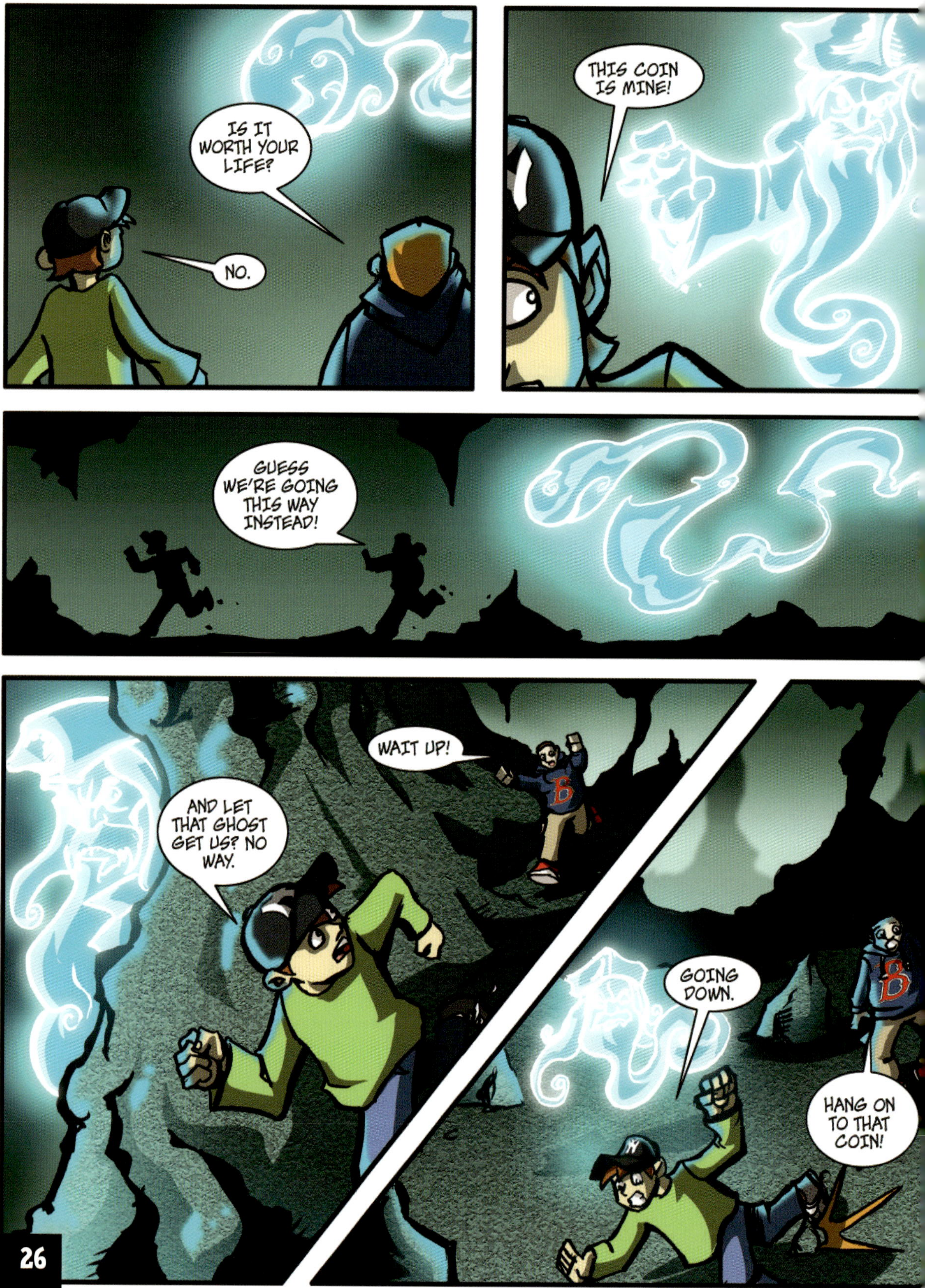
IS IT WORTH YOUR LIFE?
NO.
THIS COIN IS MINE!
GUESS WE'RE GOING THIS WAY INSTEAD!
WAIT UP!
AND LET THAT GHOST GET US? NO WAY.
GOING DOWN.
HANG ON TO THAT COIN!

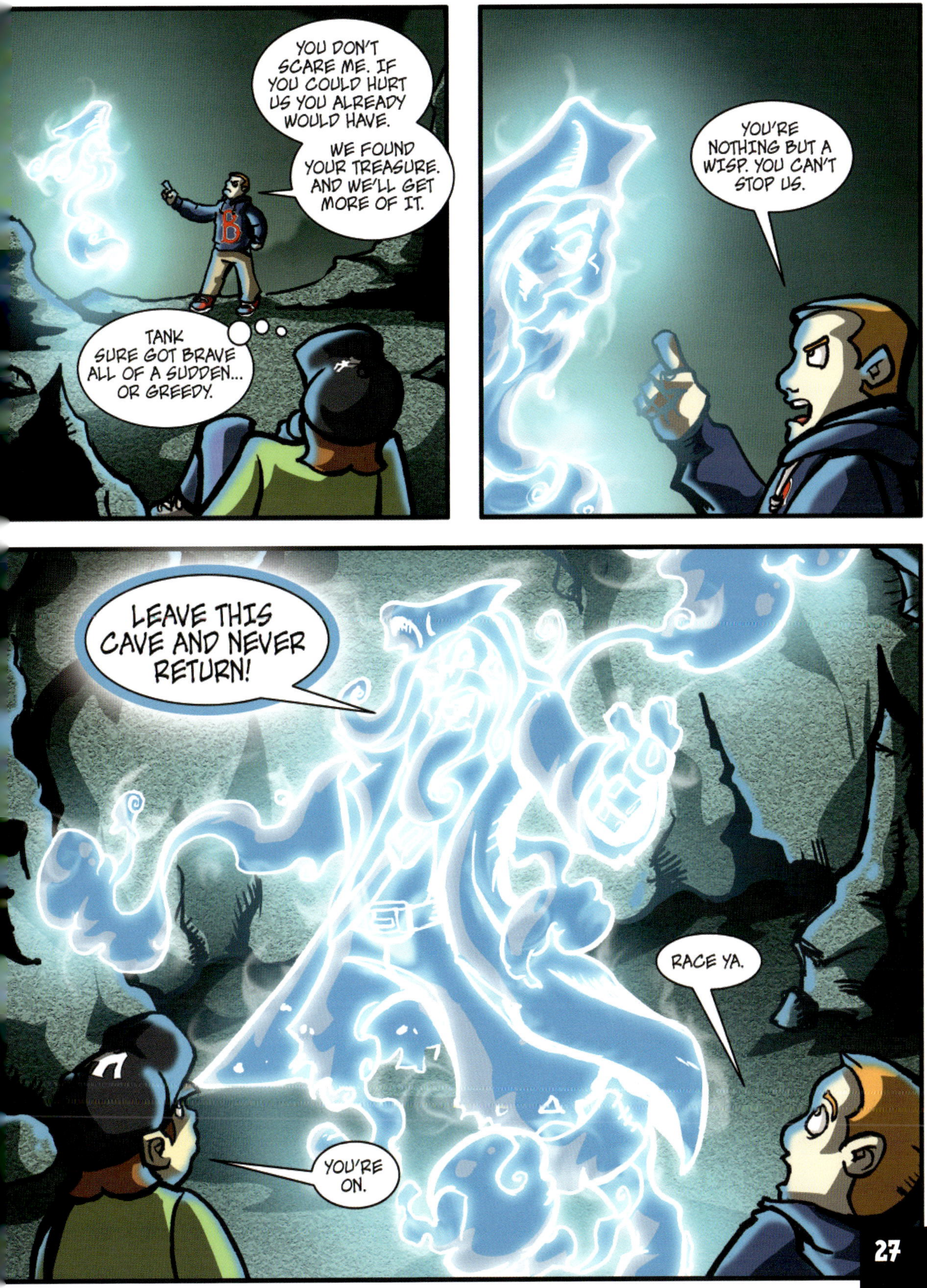
YOU DON'T SCARE ME. IF YOU COULD HURT US YOU ALREADY WOULD HAVE.
WE FOUND YOUR TREASURE. AND WE'LL GET MORE OF IT.
TANK SURE GOT BRAVE ALL OF A SUDDEN... OR GREEDY.
YOU'RE NOTHING BUT A WISP. YOU CAN'T STOP US.
LEAVE THIS CAVE AND NEVER RETURN!
RACE YA.
YOU'RE ON.

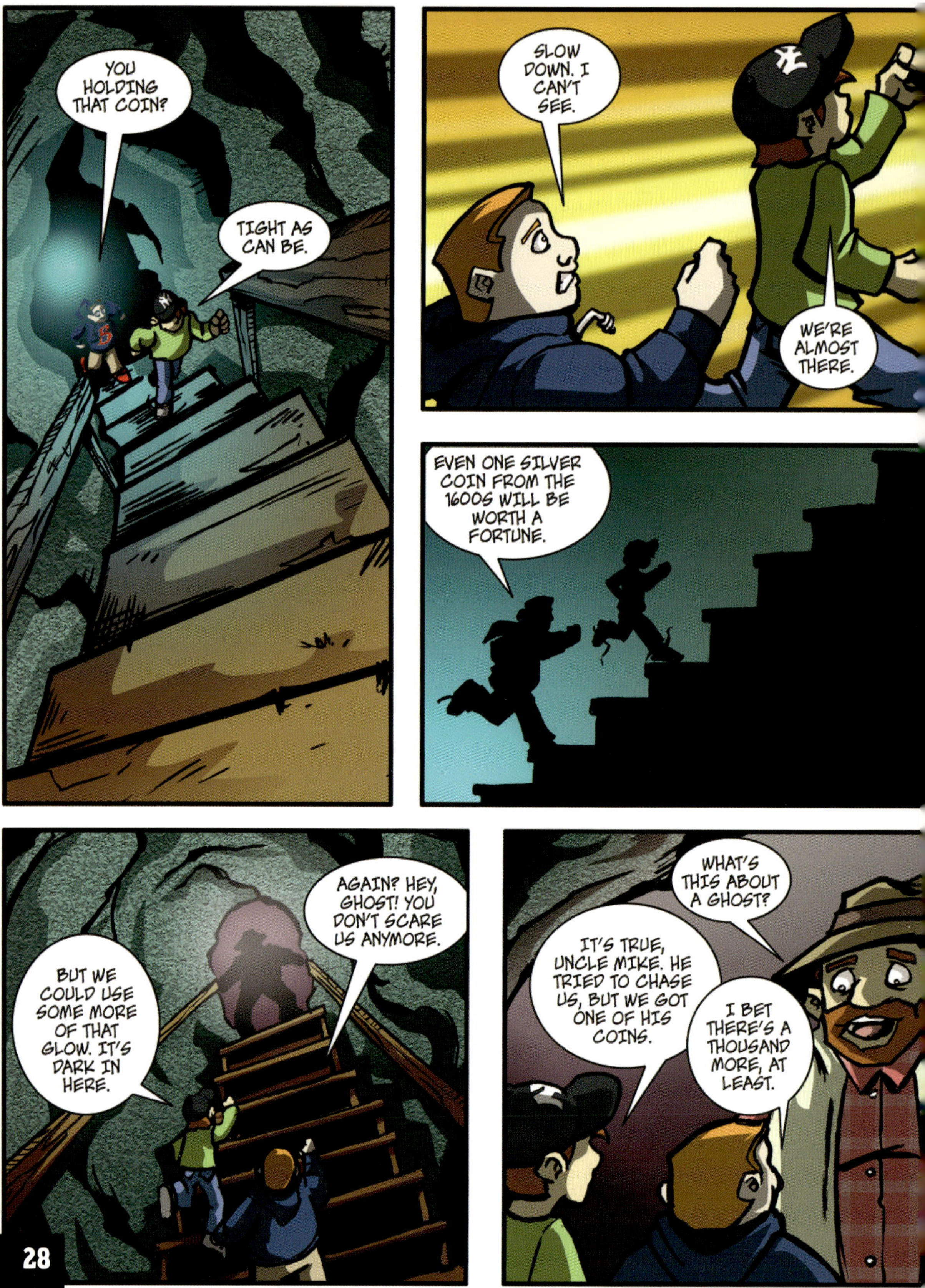
YOU HOLDING THAT COIN?
TIGHT AS CAN BE.
SLOW DOWN. I CAN'T SEE.
WE'RE ALMOST THERE.
EVEN ONE SILVER COIN FROM THE 1600S WILL BE WORTH A FORTUNE.
AGAIN? HEY, GHOST! YOU DON'T SCARE US ANYMORE.
BUT WE COULD USE SOME MORE OF THAT GLOW. IT'S DARK IN HERE.
WHAT'S THIS ABOUT A GHOST?
IT'S TRUE, UNCLE MIKE. HE TRIED TO CHASE US, BUT WE GOT ONE OF HIS COINS.
I BET THERE'S A THOUSAND MORE, AT LEAST.

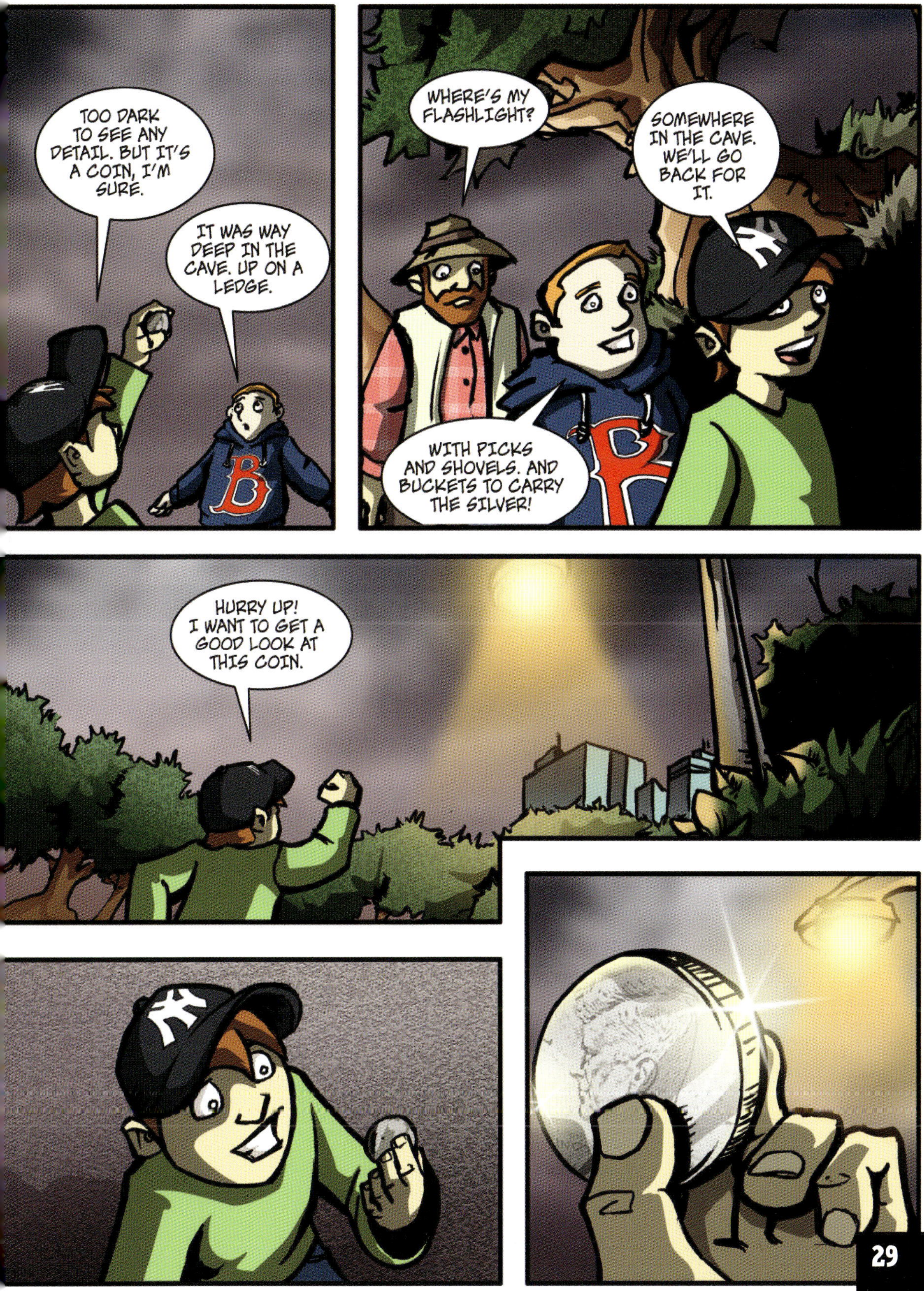

TOO DARK TO SEE ANY DETAIL. BUT IT'S A COIN, I'M SURE.
IT WAS WAY DEEP IN THE CAVE. UP ON A LEDGE.
WHERE'S MY FLASHLIGHT?
SOMEWHERE IN THE CAVE. WE'LL GO BACK FOR IT.
WITH PICKS AND SHOVELS. AND BUCKETS TO CARRY THE SILVER!
HURRY UP! I WANT TO GET A GOOD LOOK AT THIS COIN.

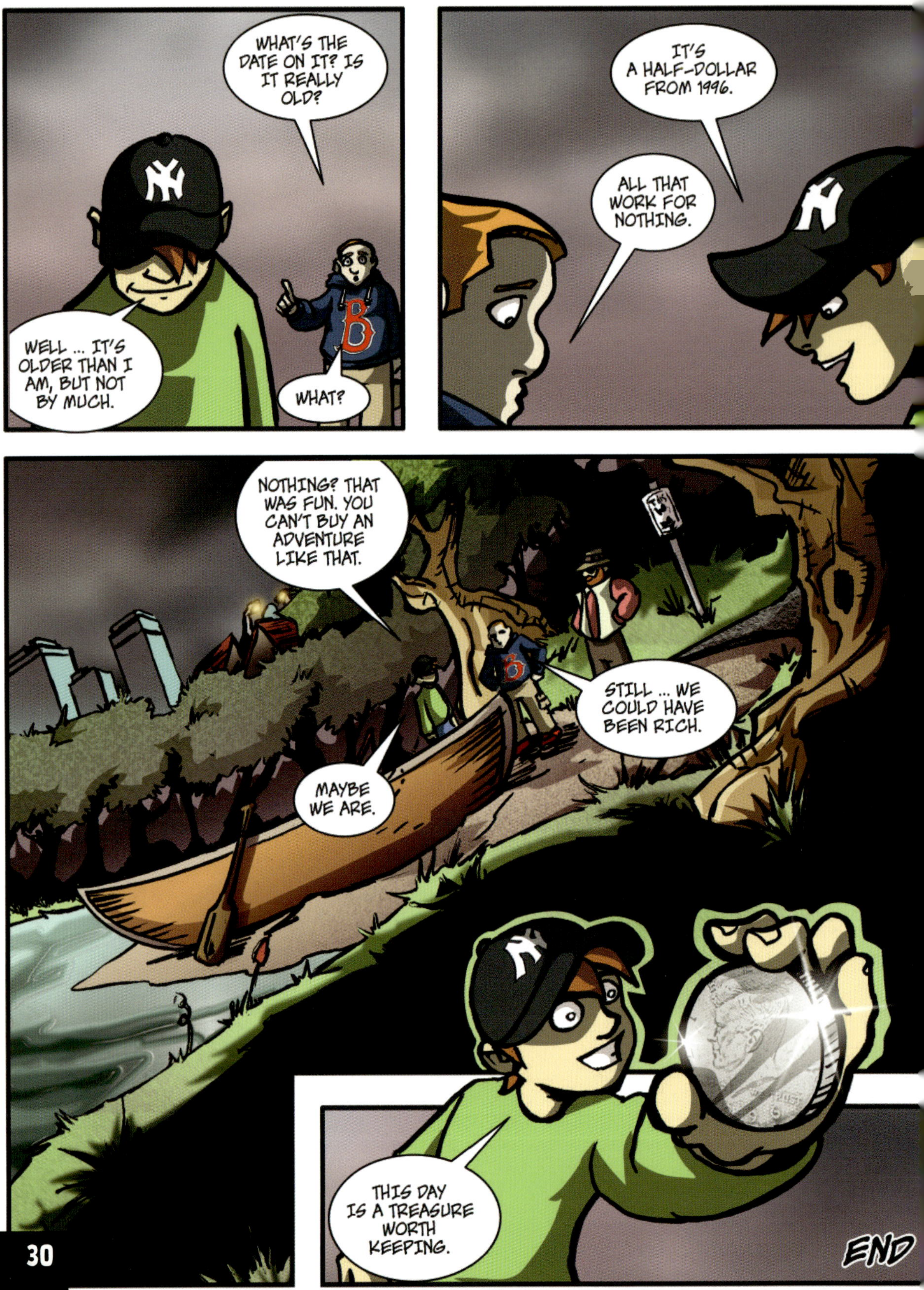
WHAT'S THE DATE ON IT? IS IT REALLY OLD?
WELL ... IT'S OLDER THAN I AM, BUT NOT BY MUCH.
WHAT?
IT'S A HALF-DOLLAR FROM 1996.
ALL THAT WORK FOR NOTHING.
NOTHING? THAT WAS FUN. YOU CAN'T BUY AN ADVENTURE LIKE THAT.
STILL ... WE COULD HAVE BEEN RICH.
MAYBE WE ARE.
THIS DAY IS A TREASURE WORTH KEEPING.
END

DUNGEON ROCK

Late one summer in the 1650s, a pirate ship sailed up the Saugus River just north of Boston, Massachusetts. After setting the anchor, four pirates rowed to shore in a smaller boat. They made their way to the nearby Saugus Iron Works.

The pirates left a note that asked for several iron items, including hatchets, shovels, and shackles. The note said the items would be paid for with silver coins. The items were delivered and paid for in secret.

It turned out that the pirate ship was being hunted by representatives of the king of England. The four pirates camped out in the woods, burying part of the ship's treasure. Three of the pirates were soon caught and arrested. The fourth man, Thomas Veal, escaped.

Veal made his way deeper into the woods and began living in a cave. It is said that he made a living as a shoemaker for several years, and that he moved at least part of the treasure to the cave.

In 1658, an earthquake buried Veal inside the cave. The cave became known as Dungeon Rock, an eternal prison for a pirate. The pirates' treasure has never been found.

The area around Dungeon Rock is now a large park called Lynn Woods Reservation. It is full of ponds, streams, and forest. Today, visitors can enter and explore Dungeon Rock.

GLOSSARY

collapse – to cave or fall in.

current – the flow of water.

hatchet – a short-handled ax often with a hammerhead to be used with one hand.

maneuver – to make changes in direction and position for a specific purpose.

navigate – to direct the course of a boat, ship, or plane.

rubble – broken pieces of rock that come from a destroyed building.

shackle – a metal band fastened around a slave's the ankle or wrist. Shackles are usually chained to the floor or wall. They prevent the slave from escaping.

WEB SITES

To learn more about Dungeon Rock, visit ABDO Group online at **www.abdopublishing.com**. Web sites about Dungeon Rock are featured on our Book Links page. These links are routinely monitored and updated to provide the most current information available.